I0625800

GAGE

TRENTON SECURITY BOOK 3

J.M. DABNEY

HOSTILE WHISPERS PRESS, LLC

Copyright © 2019 by J.M. Dabney

Hostile Whispers Press, LLC

ISBN: 978-1-947184-26-8

Cover by: Reese Dante (ReeseDante.com)

Edits by: AlternativEdits (Laura McNellis)

Proof Edit by: Stephanie Carrano

REMEMBER:

This book is a work of fiction. All characters, places, and events are from the author's imagination and should not be confused with fact. Any resemblance to persons, living or dead, events or places, is purely coincidental.

PLEASE BE ADVISED:

This book contains material that is only suitable for mature readers. It may contain scenes of a sexual nature and/or violence.

For my Readers
I can't thank everyone enough for their support in purchasing and reviewing my titles and most importantly for embracing my voices who are outside the norm.

Every Body is Worthy!

Special thanks to the people who've kicked my ass every time I think about giving up. Tracey, Stephanie, Meredith, Michelle, Laura and Jenn. I love my enablers and the unconditional support y'all show me.

NOTE TO READERS

This title contains the following triggers: Self-Harm. Suicide. Domestic Abuse. Human Trafficking. Off-Page Implied Rape.

Thank you in advance for your reviews and in taking the time to read Gage and Derrick's story.

— J.M. DABNEY

PROLOGUE

HOUSTON, TEXAS 1988

*H*ayden Gage stood outside the recruiting office hours after he'd walked across the stage of his high school auditorium and accepted his diploma. Only a few months separated him from freedom. He knew what he wanted, and he was going to escape the last seventeen years of hell. Three of them he'd fought alone without the one person who'd loved him —his mother. He struggled to remember the sound of her voice and the way her arms felt around him when she hugged him. At times, he wondered if she was just something he'd created to make his life bearable.

The day his life descended into an abyss was never far from his mind. Functioning without his mother was more than he could take and it was a struggle to keep going.

"HIDE, Hayden, don't come out until I call you." His mother's voice was soft in his ear.

The Major's face was red with rage, and the veins strained in his forehead and neck. A sure sign that the man's control had broken. He'd run to his room and hid just as she'd told him to. The crash of shattering

1

glass had forced him deeper into the tight corner between his bed and the wall. He'd just turned ten. Birthday or not, Major Dennis Gage hadn't relaxed his command. The Major was a larger than life figure in his uniform. Brutally cruel with no kind words for his wife or son, they were things to command and control, nothing more.

"What did I tell you, woman," Major yelled.

"It's his birthday. He deserves—"

The violence of a slap cut off what she'd started to say.

He'd hugged his skinny legs to his chest and tried to make himself as small as possible.

"Get your ass down here, boy."

The anger in his father's voice warred with the order from his mother to stay hidden.

"Do you want your mother to take your punishment and hers?"

Her cries drew him from his hiding space and his feet dragged on the thick carpet. He heard another punch and a high-pitched grunt. His fingertips traced the banister as he made his way downstairs.

When he entered the kitchen, his mother was bloody and bruised where she knelt on the floor. His father's hand fisted in her hair, and it seemed the only thing keeping his mother upright.

"It's time you learned how to be a man, Hayden. How to run your home. Keep your wife in her place."

He felt his bottom lip start to tremble and he kept his gaze on his mother's. Even through her pain and the blood that stained her teeth and lips, she smiled at him. She'd told him every day he could remember of his ten years that he was who she lived for and that God giving her him was her greatest joy.

"It's okay, baby, you'll—"

He ran to her as he watched her take another hit. She collapsed to the floor and hunks of her pretty hair were torn away, hanging from his father's fist.

"They need to know their place, son."

. . .

HE BLOCKED OUT THE MEMORIES. He leaned his back on a light pole as he kept his gaze on the building. His mother took every punch, slap, and kick until she was so broken that she didn't know anything else. People would think it strange, but the physical abuse came nowhere near the damage his old man's words had caused. He'd watched the black and purple bruises fade over weeks of time. The mental and emotional ones lingered so much longer. They were etched into the premature wrinkles and the silver that overtook her thick and shiny cocoa hued hair.

The Major's abuse aged her far beyond her years. No one ever noticed the slight tremble to her slender, gentle hands—the ones she wrung when her anxiety grew.

The happiest times of his life were the ones where his old man was deployed, and his childhood was normal. He needed out. He'd inherited the man's anger. It slithered beneath the surface ready to strike. He'd awakened from blackouts too often with blood-stained hands. His friends shouting behind him and attempting to pull him away from his victims.

The only way for survival or to stay out of prison was to leave it all behind. Nothing was holding him there any longer. His mother escaped three years earlier. He'd come home from school during one of the happy times, or so he'd thought.

HE'D RUN into the house and to the kitchen where his mother always waited for him. She hadn't greeted him with a hug and an I love you. He knew he was too old to accept her motherly affection, but it was the single kindness that his mother received in her life. No matter what a bastard he'd started to grow into, he'd always wanted to be the one happy thing she had.

He had dropped his bag beside the kitchen table and went in search of her. The upstairs bathroom door had stood open, and as he walked inside, he wondered why she was bathing so early. At first, he'd thought she was asleep and when he'd drawn closer, his calling out to her ceased as she bathed in a pool of crimson. Her skin was paler. He'd touched her shoulder, and her flesh was icy under his shaking hand.

His voice had shook as he'd called her name. She hadn't responded. Tears scalded his cheeks as he'd fallen to his knees to shake her harder. Screaming her name. Begging for her to wake up, but she hadn't, and he stumbled back from the tub.

He didn't know how long he'd tried to get her to wake up before he ran for the kitchen to dial 9-1-1. He'd returned upstairs, covered her body with a towel. No one needed to see her like that. He'd hugged her and buried his face against her throat. She still smelled like his mother. The sweet, comforting scent of her lotion. She'd be fine. The paramedics would make her all better. She'd wake up and smile, say she loved him—how proud she was he was her son.

That hadn't happened. Hours later, he'd sat numbly in the hospital waiting room. She'd protected him until she'd broken. He didn't care about the nurses and doctors saying they were sorry. Telling him she'd just gone to sleep.

THE ONLY PEACE his mother had ever found was in the moment of her death. His father had forbidden him to mourn. When his mother died, parts of him had as well. She was his comfort. The only person he'd ever loved. With her gone, his father turned his rage onto him. He'd taken it, but no more.

"Were you coming inside, young man?"

A man in a sharp uniform, a friendly face with deep lines and an easy smile. Black hair cut short and regulation.

"Yes, sir."

"Then come on, we'll talk while we have a cup of coffee."

He nodded as he walked through the door—this was his future. Life on his terms. He wouldn't be his old man, and he'd never break someone's spirit to the point that their only option for safety was in their last breath.

THE LITTLE BOY MUST BE CRAZY

*D*ishes rattled, and the low murmuring of conversations filled the interior as the lunch rush started to slow down at Heidi's Diner. Typically, Gage ate alone before returning to the office, but today, he hadn't turned out to be so lucky.

"How about I buy you dinner, Gage," the confident young man across the table from him asked.

He stared at the boy as if he'd lost his mind. He slowly closed his laptop and calmly leaned back in the booth. The first time he'd seen Derrick Thorpe the kid was skin and bones, skittish from years of abuse by Derrick's homophobic and racist father, the former Sheriff of Powers County, Georgia. The last time he'd allowed himself to be in the same space with Derrick, he had graduated from college. His boss, Linus, adopted Derrick and his toddler brother after the death of their father and, well, the mother hadn't fought Linus when the man demanded she sign over custody.

Today Derrick was a man in his mid-twenties, and even with the pale blond stubble, he was still as pretty as the last time he'd seen him which had occurred Christmas a year ago. He'd made his excuses and went to stay with friends for the holiday. Fighting any of the Crews to get out of a family function always turned into a lost cause, and he'd found it easier to escape.

Gage forced a chuckle and a good-natured smile at the eager boy in front of him, but he felt neither of those actions. Because his greatest hell sat across from him and there was no way he'd ever allow the boy close to him.

"Not going to happen, kid."

"Why not?" Derrick looked offended.

He wasn't fucking around with some boy with Daddy issues. No matter how much he wanted to find out what his handprint looked like on the boy's ass. Derrick wasn't for him. Age difference aside, with Derrick's history, he wouldn't let the young man find out how interested he was.

"Go find someone your own age, Derrick."

"What's this got to do with age? I'm an adult, and I think I'm old enough to know what I want."

He felt the muscles in his jaw clench. He didn't like telling people no twice. When he made a decision, it was final. This little boy was asking for a spanking. A vision of Derrick over his knee came to mind, and he banished it as quickly as it appeared. This was getting out of hand. That's why he'd avoided anything that had to do with seeing Derrick.

"And I said it wasn't happening. I don't like to repeat myself, Derrick."

Derrick's chin lowered to rest on his chest. There was a deep breath, and then Derrick looked up, his dark brown eyes shimmered with indignation.

"Yes, sir," Derrick pushed the words through clenched teeth.

Gage reached down and grabbed his laptop bag, stowing his computer inside. He didn't have time to deal with Derrick today. He had enough kids he had to deal with at work. Every time his team fucked up, he had to fix it.

He slid off the bench seat, removed his wallet from his back pocket and threw enough money on the table to cover his check, plus a tip. He rested the strap of the bag on his shoulder.

He strode toward the exit and outside. Trenton Security Headquarters was only a few blocks away, and he spent too much time trapped in his office, so any chance he got to take a walk he did. He'd hired on with Linus more years ago than he could remember, right when the company was just starting out. His military career had run its course, and he hadn't wanted to settle into a life of command after his years with his *SEAL* team.

"Pop said you were coming to dinner tonight."

He growled in his chest as Derrick walked beside him. He'd already told Linus he wasn't coming to dinner; last count was twenty. His boss and friend was determined to have Gage attend every fucking function the Crews had. He knew his team wasn't happy about him pulling back. They were a small tight crew. Except for a few freelancers they brought in, it was just the seven of them and that included their attorney, Peaches Phelps.

"Still living at home?"

"I move into my apartment at the end of the month. I can't wait, the dads are completely hovering, and Dad is the worst one."

"Hunter letting you out of his sight is shocking." Hunter, one of Linus's two husbands, was possessive of his adopted sons, even if Derrick was already seventeen when the boy moved in with them. That didn't matter to Hunter, and the man had decided his son was going to have the best life.

"Dad isn't happy. He tried to get me to agree to have a trailer moved out onto their property. I love them, but they love to try to make everything better. I've been living on my own for five years."

A reminder of Derrick's age, he'd be lying to himself if he said that was the only problem he had. No, he wanted Derrick, and what he wanted with the boy was something he wasn't going to allow to happen. Just the thought of pushing Derrick to the edge only to bring him back got him hard. All the nights he'd dreamed of fucking his boy and claiming him were a temptation that he barely resisted. He couldn't allow himself to weaken, no matter how much he wanted to do just that.

At least the kid was acting sensible and not harping on the date which made things a little easier—not much though.

"I'm sure they get it, but you know Hunter gets a little protective."

"I know, and I really appreciate it, but I'm an adult. Hunter isn't too happy with my career choice, neither is Lily, but for different reasons."

Linus' mother Lily was militantly anti-establishment and had scarcely survived with her reputation intact when her son dared marry a deputy. Now her grandson was betraying her, too. He could already see her losing her shit over that. Her meltdown over Deputy Wren was legend even years later.

"You do know Pelter looks the other way on certain things."

Derrick laughed. "Yeah, they'd have to expand the department to have enough cells for all the Crews."

"Ready to start as the newest Powers' Deputy?"

"Yes. I'm trying to not dread working for Pelter."

"He's not so bad. Linus just drives him crazy."

"That, but—"

He knew what was coming. "Derrick, you're not your father."

"Thorpe isn't my dad, he never was. My dads wanted me. They were there for everything from graduations or just when I called saying I needed them."

He turned his head to find Derrick with his hands deep in his pockets and staring down at the toes of his tactical boots.

He didn't question his actions, he raised his hand to push his fingers under Derrick's chin and forced the boy's gaze to his. "I'm sorry." He dropped his arm back to his side before he had the chance to cup Derrick's jaw and stroke his thumb over the lush curve of the man's lower lip.

"It's fine, I grew up with Thorpe, and every day was hell. I just don't like being reminded."

The misery of Derrick's expression caused him to want to rid the man of all his problems and worries, but he wasn't meant to have a boy—a partner—of his own.

He decided to change the subject to make Derrick more comfortable. "What's tonight's dinner honoring?"

"I don't know, could be my new job or something else. I hear it's going to be just the Trenton Crew. Well, maybe not Little and Poe, I think they're fighting again."

He chuckled. "When don't those two fight?" Little and Poe had a weird relationship. Who the hell married the man who kidnapped them? Apparently, Poe did.

"It's foreplay. Little pisses Poe off just for the make-up sex."

"That's true. I wonder if Poe had some Stockholm—"

Derrick's loud snort cut him off. "Little only had Poe a few hours. Little's cute, I don't know how a beast like him can be cute, but when he gets in trouble, he starts batting those lashes with his pretty green eyes and Poe is in a fucking puddle. And don't even get me started on Liv and Fielding."

"If I have to talk to Liv and hear Fielding moaning and shit in the background, I'm shoving pens in my ears."

"You gotta admit it's nice being wanted that much."

"There's more to a relationship than sex."

"Is there? And what might that be, Gage?"

He stopped and glanced over his shoulder to find Derrick watching him. The innocent little drop of his lashes and that peek of Derrick's tongue moving over his bottom lip. He clenched his hands so hard they hurt.

"My boy will know his place is on his knees beside my chair and not to be a mouthy brat who asks for a spanking."

Derrick's eyes widened, and the boy's face was flushed pink. The boy looked away and ignored him.

"Um, I have to go, gotta get home."

"Goodbye, Derrick. Please tell them I won't be attending tonight."

"Yes, s-sir."

He felt his mouth pull into a smirk at Derrick running in the opposite direction. Maybe he should've tried that approach earlier. Seemed his—fuck, not his—the boy wasn't up to playing the game Derrick started. He pivoted on his toes and continued toward Trenton Security.

He wished he could forget. He was too old for the boy, but his body didn't give a fuck. The things he wanted to do to Derrick, hearing his boy beg to be fucked was only one of them. He required a certain level of control and someone who trusted he knew what was best.

He raised his hand to rub his beard and shook his head as he breathed through his irritation. He made it this long without giving in to his desire and his baser need to dominate one of his best friend's son. He didn't want to deal with the hell Hunter, Linus and Wren would bring down on him if he decided to sully Derrick. No matter the threats, it didn't change years of wanting someone who he considered forbidden. He was right where he wanted to be in life—loved his job and the place he lived, settling in Powers was the first place he didn't feel the need to run.

His demons weren't in this town, and their memory didn't taint everything around him. Decades of nightmares muffled but not silenced, and he couldn't chance someone learning the truth about what a broken man he was. He wasn't fucking up no matter how much his brain and body screamed Derrick Thorpe was made for him.

DID GAGE WANT TO BE HIS DADDY?

*D*errick locked his bedroom door behind him and leaned back against it. He'd barely made it through dinner as Gage's words repeatedly played through his head. On his knees…did he want that with Gage? He had known since he was seventeen that he'd wanted Gage. The night Little and Wren brought him and his brother, Craig, to the Trenton Security office and he'd spotted the older stoic man, he'd lost his heart.

Gage's voice was a whiskey-smooth baritone and held so much command that he'd instantly relaxed. Gage had made him feel safe for the first time. The older man's dominant nature seemed to ground him. He'd lived his life in fear for so long that it was just normal. Almost a decade later, he still found it impossible to relax around men until he knew them. He always anticipated the first strike. The possibility of the cycle of abuse continuing frightened him, and it would become so easy to fall back into the pattern of the familiarity of it, but he refused to allow that to happen.

Away from home and his safe spaces, he'd made his masculinity unquestionable. He'd even avoided questions about his parents. What was he supposed to say? His dads, all three of them, were happily in a ménage marriage. He'd grown weary of being someone he wasn't, and although that was the main reason he'd come home, it wasn't the only one.

He sighed heavily and pushed away from the door. He strode to his bed and fell face first onto it. The years passed and his need hadn't changed. He belonged to Gage, but the older man treated him like an annoying kid. He'd tried everything to make Gage see him as a man. Nothing had worked and all that today's encounter had done was prove that he wasn't someone that Gage would want.

"You locked your door," Craig aka Pride accused.

"That means I wanted privacy." He rolled to his back and studied the stubborn expression on the twelve-year old's face. He felt like an outsider because he hadn't come to live with their new family until he was seventeen, but Pride had settled in and found himself. He was proud of his brother. Smart, confident, and knew himself. His brother could be who he was without judgment. "Practicing a new talent?"

"Bedroom doors are no problem. Raul is teaching me to pick locks."

"First pockets, now locks." He shook his head as Pride dived onto the bed and he stretched his arm out for Pride to rest his head.

"Raul said they're useful skills."

That was Pride's go-to answer for just about everything, and he wondered what his dads thought about their youngest son's mentor. Pride seemed to be readying himself to join the family business.

"You break in for a reason?"

"I kinda like these two people."

"And?" Having three Dads, then two Uncles both married to two men, ménage or poly relationships seemed natural when it's what someone grew up with. One man was just fine for him. He was greedy and longed to be the sole focus of one man.

"Is that wrong?"

"Is it wrong that our dads love each other, or that Uncle Elijah or Uncle Pelter love their husbands?"

"No, but it's a boy and a girl."

"Do you want to tell me who?" He already knew or in his gut, he'd always known. Ricky, Sawyer, and Pride were inseparable for years. Like with all the Crew Hellions, they were insanely protective of each other. He'd noticed a few who he already predicted their closeness would turn into more as they reached their teens or twenties.

"Not really."

"Pride, you're my brother, I love you, and I'll support you. As long as what people do together is consensual and safe, then if you like these two people, I'll be there. Maybe it'll be confusing now at twelve, but if sometime in the future you want to tell them, do it."

"You've never brought a boyfriend home. Don't you want one?"

"I want one a lot, but sometimes what we want isn't what we get. Maybe one day."

As with Pride's usual modus operandi he drifted into silence. His brother tended to drift into a world of his own. He turned his head to brush a kiss to Pride's temple and then brought his attention back to the ceiling. His own thoughts were too chaotic. For almost a decade, all he'd wanted was Gage to see him as a man. To have all his fantasies of having Gage as his own come true. Unfortunately, Gage still saw him as that broken, seventeen-year-old who needed saving.

"Pride, come on, bedtime. You have school in the morning, and you still have homework. I'm not dealing with another parent-teacher conference, and you're not hacking into the system to change your grades."

Pride groaned and rolled off the bed as Hunter yelled through the door. He told his brother goodnight, and when he left, Pride locked the door behind him. His brother was smart as hell. He'd wanted to learn everything Hunter did, and in hindsight, he believed their dad might regret teaching Pride. His baby brother had a lot of skills a kid shouldn't have. Pure, another member of Trenton Security said Pride was a natural when it came to sniper practice. What had they expected when they'd adopted them and Pride spent more time at Trenton Security than anywhere else? Pride had quite the education.

He'd had two goals in life, to prove he wasn't like his biological father and to make Gage his, but he'd only half succeeded at one of them. How did he get the older man to look at him like the people in his extended family looked at their partners? He hadn't believed love existed until he'd met his adoptive parents' extended family. All the devotion was there for all to see. The touches just to be able to feel someone and take comfort in their presence.

As much as he wanted love like that, only one man would do. He'd worked his ass off to come back to Powers to prove to Gage that he was a man. The age difference didn't bother him, but he also had never seen Gage with anyone or heard anyone talk about someone Gage was dating. He'd acted like a starving man for any scrap of information. He'd held his breath waiting to hear about a boyfriend or someone more important.

His heart soared every year that passed, and Gage remained single.

A job in law enforcement wasn't where he'd seen himself. He actually thought he might take on a position at Trenton Security. He'd gone to college, received his criminal justice degree, and applied to the academy. They told him he could be anything, but he wanted to come back to Powers and prove that he wasn't anything like the man who'd fathered him.

Pelter reluctantly hired him and only because of who he was, Linus Trenton's adopted son. He hadn't changed his name from Thorpe to Trenton, but he'd wanted that. Yet being connected to the Trenton name caused as many problems as Thorpe. Linus hadn't made many friends in law enforcement during the man's days as a cop. The Trenton Crew weren't the most law-abiding people around. They had a way of twisting laws to suit their purposes, and with the help of Peaches Phelps, they rarely paid for their *crimes*.

He spent the first seventeen years of his life afraid and covered in bruises or ignored. Too many years he'd watched the murderous rage in Thorpe's eyes as he spewed hate and he was one of those people his father hated. Out of terror, he'd denied who he was, dated girls in high school, fumbled through make-out sessions. Fingered his date until she came and imagined her hand around his cock was harder and rougher. Shame had nearly killed his spirit.

His thoughts depressed him and then suddenly another horrible thought hit him, what if Gage was straight? Just because he worked around gay and bisexual men and called them his best friends didn't mean he was gay. What if the man of his dreams was straight but just went along with the boy talk to embarrass or scare him off? He groaned as he covered his face. Of course, Gage wouldn't be offended—the older man didn't find anything offensive about being considered gay.

Fuck, just what he needed, falling in love with a man who would never love him back. One that would eventually find the woman of his dreams and he'd have to watch Gage date, fall in love and marry a woman who would have the right to love and touch him in return.

He felt the tears against the pads of his fingers and slipping down his cheeks. His heart broke with that one realization and thought about having to move on while trapped in the same town as Gage. His only saving grace was he'd never told anyone about his crush, but he'd asked Gage out. The man probably had a good laugh about that. All his dreams shattered and he wondered what the hell he was going to do—how was he going to get over a love that would never be reciprocated.

MARKERS CALLED IN

*T*he stinging burn of the razor danced across his skin in a lethal waltz. The pain pushed the blackness of his thoughts away. The sallower complexion of his mother's bloodless face. The emptiness of her glassy eyes. He imagined what she'd felt in those last moments. Did she feel peace knowing her pain was at an end? Did she rejoice that her body would never bear the marks of his father's fists—his fingertips?

He pictured her smiling as she had when she looked at him. As if her happiness was a gift that he gave her just by existing. Next line, exactly an inch from the one before. His forearm was a twisted landscape. Each mark told a story—a thought of violence. A tear shed in weakness. Every hard-on caused by the cute boy or man he'd met since he learned he was gay. Reminders of why he had to be alone. Warnings of the monster hidden away, birthed by the violence of his father.

Almost forty years of cuts. Of tales told in the flesh. Accepting the pain. A hiss pushed past his compressed lips as the third cut went deeper than the last. Was his mother at peace? Did she find happiness on the other side? Did she burn in Hell for her last act of escape or was there nothing beyond this life? All he wanted to do was find that one vein. He traced it with the edge of his sanitized razor. All it would take is one second of increased strength.

All of this was his touchstone, and he dragged his fingertips over his flesh as if they told the stories of his agony. Each cut was proof of the danger he was to those he would love—the man he would destroy. He refused to be the reason his partner/husband would end up in a tub of bloodied water.

He pushed, felt his flesh split, and sighed in relief as it all flowed away. All he had to do was sink it deeper, fall asleep, but again he was a failure. He tossed the razor aside, cleaned and dressed his wounds to make sure they wouldn't bleed through the expensive linen of his dress shirt. Just one more day, another twenty-four hours and he'd be able to do it again. He allowed himself to cut once a day and no more.

He cleaned up his mess and tossed the bloody gauze in the trash, along with the razor with the cardboard guard back in place. The ache on his forearm barely registered as he grabbed his stuff and headed for the door. As soon as he closed it behind him, his phone rang, and he cursed. They better not need him at seven in the morning.

After digging his phone out, the name on the display made him frown—they weren't scheduled for their weekly check-in for another few days. He connected the call.

"Hey, man, what's up?"

"I need you. I'm calling in my marker."

The panic was clear in Alex's voice. He'd known the man for nearly three decades, and even in the heat of battle, he'd never heard that tone before.

"Whatever you need, no marker needed."

"Cameron went missing forty-eight hours ago. She was on vacation with a friend's family in Miami. One minute she was there, man, and then they said she was gone."

Cameron was fourteen, good kid, and never been in trouble.

No history of running away. She was a beautiful, petite blonde that looked younger than her age. All the shit that could make her disappear ran through his head at lightspeed, and he liked none of the options.

"Missing person report?"

"Filed as soon as they called. I went down there. No one saw a fucking thing."

Alex was more low-key than him, nothing fazed the man, so hearing the panic, he had to get Alex under control. He needed Alex's head on straight if they were going to find Cameron.

"Dude, how soon can you get here?"

"I'm already on my way. Anywhere I can land a private jet?"

"I'll clear it with Pelter. He has a private strip."

"You think he'll let me back into Powers?"

"Don't worry about it. Just get here, and we'll find her. Let me know an ETA, and I'll be out there to pick you up."

"Gage, if something happened to her…"

"No one remains breathing. Nowhere they can hide."

"Thank you."

"Just get your head on straight, and we'll figure it out."

"I know, I'll be there in three hours."

He disconnected the call, and it didn't take long to make calls to everyone he needed including Peaches. She could get through any red tape for them. His heart kicked up its pace, and he couldn't even imagine what Alex was going through. He'd called Cameron his niece since before she was born and he had the honor of being her godfather. His best friend lived for that girl.

The trip across town from his place on the outskirts of Powers took half the time it normally would. He was swiping his card just as the rest of the team came up behind him.

"What's the situation? You don't call in a nine-one-one ever," Linus was asking as they took the elevator to the third floor with the offices and conference room.

"Forty-eight hours ago, Alex's daughter went missing on

vacation with friends in Miami. He went down to investigate himself, and no one knew shit. Alex called in a favor, and I need y'all on this."

"Definitely. What do we know?" Peaches took her usual spot on the tabletop and crossed her legs under her hippie skirt.

No one would think the woman was the best defense attorney in the country by looking at her. Heavily tattooed, hippie clothes, and laidback nature, and completely fucking ruthless.

"Nothing, a missing person report was filed."

"I'm on it." Hunter was talking and already on the move to his cave of an office.

The hacker was the best, and he wouldn't even attempt to know what the man did for them.

"You do know what the possibility is, right?"

Of course, Raul would go for the throat, and he wanted to snarl but held it in. "Yeah, I know the possibility, and if that's the case, we have less than thirty-six hours to find her or we might never. I can't deal with that option."

"Man, I'm just saying, I know it's your best friend's kid, but we have to be realistic."

"Raul," Pure growled.

"What?"

"Shut the fuck up."

If he wasn't so pissed, he'd almost laugh at the murderous look on Pure's handsome face. The way Raul hid flipping off the other man by scratching his nose with his middle finger made him shake his head. Everyone was right, those two just needed to fuck and get it over with. Raul was already whipped.

"I was just about to bend one of my boys over my desk, and I get an emergency text. This better be fucking good," Pelter growled as he stormed into the room.

"Sorry?" he asked.

"No, you're not. So, what the fuck is up?" Pelter asked.

"Alex." Pelter rolled his eyes at Gage's attempt to fill him in. "Alex's daughter disappeared while on vacation."

Pelter's flippant response to Alex's name disappeared as the man's face went emotionless at the thought of a missing child.

"You need me to make inquiries?" Pelter asked.

"I'd owe you, man."

"Gage, you won't owe me shit, family doesn't hold markers."

For the first time since he got Alex's call, he relaxed. He glanced around the room at his teammates. Livingston's big body was positioned next to the door looking like he hadn't slept all night, which he probably hadn't as he was on an assignment with Little. Little was tapping away on his laptop, strangely silent. Even with his *SEAL* Team, he hadn't felt as if he belonged except with Alex. They'd bonded during *BUD/s* training. Alex was the first person who had made him feel as if he wasn't a fuck up and was the only person who knew of his past.

"Gage, can I talk to you in private?" Hunter asked from the doorway.

He left everyone behind and met Hunter in the hallway. "What's up?"

"I did an initial search, don't ask me where, I won't tell you, but I did a quick search for the Miami/Dade area. There's four small auctions taking place in the next seven days."

"Is the…" He cleared his throat and tried to ask again.

"Products not listed, but information is coming in on the night of the auctions. I know someone who could patch me in under legit invites to the auctions. I'll need images to check if any of them is Alex's daughter."

"Do we have to wait? If she is going to be a part of one of these auctions, we could lose her."

"Gage, you're talking about human trafficking. We have signals bouncing all over the fucking globe. I'm great, but even I can't track them instantly. I'll have to run programs to trace them back to a source. If I could focus on one, that's easy, but we have hundreds."

He dropped his chin to his chest and placed his hands on his hips. Hunter didn't deserve his anger, but his frustration wasn't making it easy. This fucking country was founded on people being bought and sold like fucking cattle. All this bullshit shouldn't even be a thing.

"If she's sold, you can track the bidder?"

"Definitely. But again, it takes time, and right now, we have very little."

"Do what you have to do."

"I'll leave you to tell everyone."

Hunter turned and headed back to his office. He stood there taking a moment to compose himself until he could reenter the conference room.

What the fuck was he going to tell Alex?

TWO AND A HALF HOURS LATER, he arrived at the airstrip with Pelter just as the small jet was touching down. Alex exited, looking twice his age and his dark blond hair mussed.

"Hey, Alex, wish this was under better circumstances."

"Don't lie, Pelter, I remember you trying to arrest me."

"Yeah, yeah, I'll set your pilot up with a place to crash, and you and Gage take my truck." Pelter didn't linger.

He was thankful for the privacy.

"Gage, it's not good news is it?"

"Hunter found out about some auctions taking place in the area where Cam disappeared. I can't say that's what it is. We might need to go to Miami for some old-fashioned investigating."

"I searched every fucking morgue in a hundred miles of where she disappeared. Went in and looked at every blonde girl laying on a fucking slab, man. They looked away for a matter of minutes, that's all it took for my baby to be gone. Margo is losing her mind. She's still in Florida. Said she'd stay on the cops' asses."

"We'll find her, I—"

"Don't promise me. We know how this shit works. My baby could be a cold case with nothing but a moldy file with a missing person's report."

"Alex, how much shit have we been through?"

"This isn't a mission, man, this is Cameron. I can't be objective."

"We'll go back to the office, see what everyone came up with and then we'll talk about our options."

"Are we going to talk about why you're wearing long sleeves in eighty degrees?"

"No, no we're not."

He hated the coldness of his voice and left Alex standing there as he pivoted. He strode to the driver's side without a backward glance. Danger existed when others knew someone's secrets. He didn't need Alex jumping his ass for something that wasn't the other man's business. He got in the driver's seat and slammed the door. He didn't have to wait long before Alex took the spot beside him.

"You have to talk about it sometime, Gage."

"That's where you're wrong, Alex, there isn't anything to talk about."

"We'll revisit this after we find Cam."

He didn't give a fuck, just started the vehicle and reversed onto the gravel road, then changed gear to head for the office. His life was his own, and he didn't require anyone's validation. They'd find Cameron, and it would be life as usual, at least for him. He had no illusions that they'd get Cameron back the way she was before. His best friend knew it too. By any means necessary, they'd get her back.

WHERE WAS GAGE HIDING?

*G*age was missing in action or maybe just hiding from him because he hadn't seen Gage since the failed attempt to ask the older man out. His insecurities ridiculed him and told him that Gage was keeping his distance on purpose. Although, the dads and most of the Crews were strangely quiet. Wren and Cam were having secret conversations. They didn't keep secrets from each other, so it was starting to make him nervous. Especially the Trenton Crew not in the same location, where one went, they all followed. No man was ever left behind, but he didn't know how much authority he had to ask questions.

He was sure he could get the information from Grandma Peaches. She was overly protective, and if something went down, she'd know details. Gage had taken himself out of the field the last few years which made him worry with the sudden disappearance.

A heavy breath was pushed past his lips as he leaned back against the counter in his new apartment. He'd taken possession a bit early, and he already missed the chaos of home. It was the same while he was away at college and then the academy, there was a lot of fighting and occasional danger, but they also laughed. No one ever worried if they had someone at their six, it was just a given.

He sipped his coffee and grimaced—he never made it strong enough. Hunter and Linus always made it just right. He had two days off in his rotation before he took the night shift. His life felt empty, and he tried to place where it started, maybe he'd masked it with the busyness of school and training. After that, it was work and the overwhelming presence of his family and friends.

Twenty-six shouldn't feel so alone or old, but he felt as if he'd lived two lives. The one before the Crews took him and Pride in, and the current life. For seventeen years, he'd lived in a constant state of fear. Learned the art of concealing bruises and pain, pretending that he wasn't dying inside. One night had changed all that when he'd seen Little and Wren outside his bedroom window. He'd found family and peace...safety he'd never thought to experience.

Gage would be a nice bonus, but after thinking about the day at the diner, he realized Gage said the things he had to shock him —to warn him away. In a matter of seconds, the one thing he'd dreamed of for years died as a possibility. Maybe it was time for him to grow up and attempt to find someone who wanted him. Gage had never shown an interest in him, and everyone had their first heartbreak sooner or later. He'd experienced a milestone in being human, that was all.

"Derrick, you home?"

He groaned as Hunter called from the living room. He'd given his dads an extra key for emergencies.

"Hey, Dad."

"Hey, baby boy. Are you drinking tea?"

"No, coffee why?" he asked as he lifted his clear mug and snorted as he could almost see through the liquid.

"I've taught you how to do it, how many times?"

He eased to the side as his dad took over. Hunter was a few

inches taller than his almost six-foot height, and around twice as broad. The big man was a champion at Dad Hugs. His dad's long, dark hair had more gray in it than he remembered. It was still odd that the men he called Dads weren't much older than him. There was less than a decade between him and Hunter.

With a shock, he realized his cheeks hurt from smiling.

"Dad?"

"Yeah?" Hunter asked without looking away from carefully measuring coffee grounds.

"Did I ever tell you and the dads how much I appreciated y'all taking me in when you really didn't have to? I was already seventeen."

Hunter turned his head and gave him a soft, loving smile. "I loved you and your brother from the moment I saw you, I couldn't imagine not calling you my son."

He dropped his chin to his chest to attempt to hide his tears.

"Don't hide emotion, I don't care what you were taught before, but emotion doesn't make you weak."

He nodded but refused to look at Hunter again. It had taken so many years to erase the bullshit his biological family had taught him. It seemed like forever before he could say he was gay with pride. His internalized homophobia was the hardest to overcome. He'd hid it a long time when he'd gone off to school. Denied it while training at the academy just to be able to fit. Being home had felt like the only safe space to be himself.

"Can I ask you a question and not get the run around?"

"Of course," Hunter said as he finished up starting a fresh pot of coffee.

"What's going on? Gage is MIA, Wren and Cam are acting weird, and there's a lot of tension going through the Crews. That normally means a big crew mission is happening."

"You remember Alex, right?"

He nodded. Alex was Gage's best friend and helped on a few

operations for Trenton when they needed an extra man. He thought Alex might miss the action of his Team days.

"His daughter Cam disappeared about a week ago. Gage and him had to take off to Florida to follow up a few leads. You know we get a bit antsy when one of us is out of pocket."

He got that, and from what he'd heard and seen, Alex could take care of whatever, but the fact Alex was Gage's only backup made him nervous. A young girl disappearing brought up dozens of possibilities and none of them were comforting in the least.

"Are they checking in?"

"Of course, we're all working on it. We're just doing it from home."

"Leads on where she is yet?"

"No, we thought she was placed in a private auction. I patched in through a legit invite to about three of them, and we found someone who got in to check out a manifest of items."

"Y'all kill me when you talk about people as products... manifest and items."

"Sorry, it might sound cold, but sometimes it makes things easier, at least outwardly. It's Gage's niece, and it has all of us on edge. We're ignoring the elephant in the room."

"You mean that she may already be dead?"

"Try not to say that too loudly around Gage or Alex. We've seen some cold bastards in our days, but Gage and Alex as a team, it's terrifying. Even Liv is walking a wide circle around those two."

Wow, his uncle Liv had lived for the most dangerous jobs for decades. Death didn't frighten him because he hadn't possessed anything to live for until the big, scarred man met Fielding. Liv and Fielding were damn near the perfect couple, and Liv couldn't tell his boy no about anything. The man had finally had someone to live for, but Liv still took too many chances. To know the Death Wish Junkie wasn't engaging the danger of Gage told him enough about the seriousness of the situation.

He crossed his arms over his lean chest and dropped them when he reached for the coffee Hunter poured for him. The first sip was Heaven, strong yet smooth without a bitter burnt taste.

"Is Gage okay?"

"Except for his niece missing, he's the same as always. We're getting daily check-ins, and Peaches hasn't been called to defend them, so it can't be all bad yet."

"I know I'm not on the team, but I worry about everyone, keep me in the loop at least unofficially. If y'all need help or anything I'm there."

"I know, Derrick, but nothing about this is official, and we're constantly breaking laws."

He laughed and shook his head—the Crews had a bit of a spectrum of gray when it came to laws. If it could be justified, did that really mean it was illegal, or at least that's what the Trenton philosophy was, and they weren't ashamed.

"Why didn't y'all offer me a job?"

Part of him had assumed they would after he'd come home but not once had they mentioned him coming onboard.

"Because the only reason you became a deputy was to prove something to this town. We don't think it's necessary, but that's what you want. You make your own decisions, Derrick. When you're ready, there's a spot always open."

The tension he'd unknowingly held onto seemed to ease away. His dads' approval meant everything to him because it was something that he'd never had before them. He talked with Hunter another hour and let Hunter interrogate him over whether he was eating and sleeping enough. When the man asked if he was seeing anyone, he avoided the question. What was he supposed to say? That the person he wanted looked at him as nothing more than a kid—a pest.

Hunter hugged him, and then he showed him to the door. When he closed the door, he leaned back against it with a sigh.

That the man he loved found him so lacking hurt, but he was

used to being unwanted. For seventeen years, he'd believed he lived on borrowed time, one beating would go too far. He remembered as if it were yesterday what the barrel of a gun felt like pressed between his eyes. One bullet in the chamber of Thorpe's service revolver. The sound of the hammer being pulled back. The click of the empty chamber. It always stopped before the fatal shot, but he'd waited for the day his old man didn't stop.

He pushed away from the door and went to make another cup of coffee, maybe something to eat. He was going to make sure he enjoyed his few days off and try not to fall victim to the past.

THEY'RE NO CLOSER TO FINDING HER

*G*age poured himself the last cup of coffee in the pot and started another one. They were no closer to finding Cameron, and the more days that passed, the more haggard Alex looked. Neither of them were eating enough to sustain them. Sleeping in shifts as they went over report after report. Hunter sent them every piece of information he could dig up. He pushed the *Brew* button, then scratched at the fresh scars on his forearm. Counting them as he would his breaths to bring him back to the present.

He had thought that the urge to cut would lessen as he grew older. Trenton and Powers became his home, and with it, he'd wrongly assumed the nightmares would go away. That he'd find normalcy and it was so far from his reality. He still needed the pain and the thin scarred marks to keep the monster at bay. He feared he wouldn't come back from the precipice or the next blackout. Or that he'd awaken once again with blood on his hands, but this time with a victim no longer breathing at his feet.

His phone vibrated in his pocket shocking him out of his thought. The phone was put on silent a few hours before to keep from waking Alex. He dug it from his back pocket and checked the screen, then connected the call.

"Hey, Hunter, what ya got for me?"

"We have a complication."

That wasn't what he wanted to hear. They were already passed the deadline of finding her, and he didn't need any more fuck ups. Alex and him were barely holding on to their sanity. He'd found as more time passed, they snapped at each other. The only thing he could do was remember that this was harder on Alex than him.

"When don't we have one?"

"That is true. Little received a tip a few hours ago, and I checked it out. Three days from today there's a meeting at a private estate. I backtracked some IP addresses to some of the top businessmen and politicians on the east coast."

"You said there wasn't another auction going down."

"It's not an auction. It appears someone arranged for party favors and while this might be on the up and up, it's something."

When his brain should've thought positive about everything being legit; his pessimism and stress took it to a much darker place. His chest seized at what that meant. They'd pass the people around, and at the end of the party, they'd find themselves buried in a mass grave. Those would be the lucky ones—the others would be purchased at a reduced price and become some fucker's sex slave and then be disposed of when they had served their purpose.

"Is there any way you can get me in?"

"I'm working on it."

"Work faster."

"Gage, I know you're under stress, but I'm telling you, if you don't keep your shit together you have no chance of finding her."

He tried to keep himself under control, but the anger he was always weighted down by threatened to consume him. He clenched his fist on the counter and tried to breathe through the rage.

"I'm going to build you a new identity and see if we can get you noticed. There's a facilitator in charge of invitations. There's an entire vetting process, and there's only a few slots open. I already sent an inquiry as you to get the process started."

"How long?"

"Twenty-four hours. You'll need to do some shopping, and I'm sorry to say you're going to need a boy. If not, you're going to be expected to play with other toys."

Hunter was right that it would be easier to avoid participating if he already had someone with him. Someone other than Alex because he couldn't guarantee his friend would remain calm with the possibility of Cameron so close. To be honest, he didn't know if he'd handle it any better than Alex. He needed someone who could keep him grounded.

"Find someone to go with me, call in favors if you need to."

"You going to complain about whoever we send?"

"A naturally submissive backup would be preferred. I'd rather not fight with my supposed sub and draw attention."

"Once your new identity is in place, and connections are made, we'll inform you where to meet your backup. We just have to find the right one."

They finished discussing the details. Then he disconnected the call.

"Was that news?"

He glanced up as Alex stepped out of his room. His friend was dressed in nothing but pajama bottoms. At almost fifty, the man was in amazing shape, although, his wavy, dirty blond body hair was liberally streaked with silver. He poured Alex a mug of coffee as he tried to figure out how to explain the plan.

"Yeah, Hunter is building me a new identity and finding me backup. There's a party in upstate New York on an isolated estate. Hunter's working on getting me an invite."

"Why do you need backup? I'm right fucking here, man."

"Alex, I know that, but can you tell me you won't lose your shit while we're in there?"

He knew the answer Alex would give him. Yet, he waited for the man to think it through. Alex was the most level-headed man he'd met in his life, and as much as he hated not having Alex as backup, he also understood that Alex wouldn't make it as his partner inside. Alex might not think he was very alpha male, but his best friend couldn't play the sub/boy role.

The moment the realization hit Alex he saw the man deflate. The man fell onto one of the bar stools and buried his face in his hands, then Alex lifted his head. Alex's eyes were glassy with unshed tears.

"But, man, I can't just sit on the sidelines. You can't leave me out of this."

"I'll need someone to watch my back. Be my contact on the outside. Hunter is going to send the information to me. More than likely, I'll get Raul and Pure. Raul won't like it, but Pure's mine inside."

"Raul's going to kill you as slow as possible."

For the first time in days, he laughed with genuine amusement. Pure was the best option. He was soft-spoken and sweet, a bit chunky, but he'd never met a more ruthless sniper. His teammate, with a little coaching, could pull off the sub routine perfectly. Firstly, they had to get Raul under control. Pure was an idiot not to see Raul's interest because the Latino bounty hunter already acted like he'd pissed on his territory. He couldn't have Raul growling every time Gage had to put his hands on Pure.

"He'll have to show some control. I have to make a trip to the shop. In a week, I'm going to walk into a mansion of possible sadists with no rules, but I have to protect Pure from unwanted attention."

"You can put—"

"I know, I'll get a plain collar just to get through this op."

"Do you think it'll go that far?"

He was hoping he wouldn't need to push Pure's limits. Not only was Pure his teammate, but his friend as well. He wasn't sure Pure's vow of chastity was just about waiting for the right one or if something deeper was at play—some sort of trauma. He wouldn't make Pure uncomfortable for anything in the world. He'd dreamed of the day he would've found his boy, but it was a fantasy he lived in his weak moments. How things would've been different if he wasn't so damaged. If a part of him was capable of love, then maybe he would've felt worthy.

"Hope not, but I swear, man, I'll find her whatever means necessary."

"I know. All I can think is what she's going through. Have they already touched her, is she hurt, or cold? My brain is playing out every scenario there is, and none of the endings are coming out in my baby's favor. I gave up the Navy to spend time with her. To learn the young woman that she was so quickly growing in to. This is my fault. I should've told her she couldn't—"

"Alex." His voice was sharper than he meant it to be. "She could have easily been walking down the sidewalk in y'all's neighborhood and been snatched. You and Margo can't blame yourselves for this. I'm gonna run out, get what I need, and I'll be back in an hour."

He reluctantly left Alex to run his errand. He hated being away from his team—the disconnect was too draining. And as much as he felt as if Alex were a brother, it wasn't the same. When he left the Navy, he'd felt adrift until he'd found Trenton Security. In Powers, he could almost pretend he was normal. He knew he'd started to pull away from his team. That was involuntary. His brain misfired, and instantly he retreated, but it was too late to pretend he didn't feel at home with his extended family and team.

His life was a countdown to when he'd wear out his welcome.

What would they say if they saw his forearms or torso—his body hair hid most of the ugliness of scar tissue. Not all of them self-inflicted. He was a landscape of stories, not all of them tragic. Some of them related his proudest moments. A teammate saved. A tragedy averted. He wasn't broken enough not to realize that he'd done good things in his life, but as with any situation, the bad always overshadowed the good. A praise ruined by a chastisement for a silly mistake. And while he knew good and evil defined a person in the eyes of everyone else, life was about traveling a road forked and blocked. There wasn't only one clear path, but thousands of possibilities, and all he had to do was figure out the right one for him.

THEY NEEDED HIM FOR AN ASSIGNMENT

*G*etting called to Trenton Head Quarters in Powers was like being summoned to the principal's office. He remembered when he rebelled and almost flunked out of his Sophomore year of college. Linus had called and told him a date and time. The man's voice had dared him to disobey. Pelter was his boss, and he didn't remember doing anything that would bring his dads' wrath down on him.

Why did he feel like a kid again and ready to be grounded? He waved his keycard over the panel next to the elevator and took a deep breath as he waited for the car. The cables vibrated, and the doors clicked then smoothly opened. He hesitated for a moment before stepping inside and pushed the button for the top floor. His breathing picked up its pace, and he focused on slowing it down as he ascended.

He kept his gaze on the mirrored back wall, and the car stopped, jarring his body slightly. While he never feared that his three dads would hurt him or Pride in any way, they were so confident and capable, bringing out the best in each other. He never felt like he'd lived up to their expectations. They always told him how proud they were of everything he'd accomplished. They praised his milestones no matter how small.

"You going to hide in there all night?"

He spun on his toes to find Livingston staring at him with his usual bored expression. Liv was leaning against the wall beside the open door and his big hand barring the sliding panels from closing. The severely scarred man had made him nervous from the minute he'd met him, but he'd learned there was more to Liv than he'd let people see. Liv had changed so much since the man met his husband, Fielding. It was as if all the pieces had clicked into place for Liv when the man had claimed his boy.

"You know what's going on and are they going to disown me?"

Liv scoffed. "Like your dads would think of getting rid of you. Linus and Pelter are waiting for you in the conference room."

"Shit."

"Get your ass in there. We're on a tight timeframe."

Those words got him moving, and as he strode down the long hallway, he darted a look into Hunter's office to find the chair in front of the bank of monitors empty. As he closed the distance to the open door, he not only found Pelter and Linus, but also Hunter, Pure and Raul in the conference room. As soon as he entered all eyes were on him.

"Close the door," Linus ordered.

He did as he was asked and he shoved his hands into his pockets to hide the slight tremor. "What have I done?"

"Take a seat and relax, you're going to be here a while," Linus said as he motioned for him to sit.

Fuck, he removed his hands from his pockets and sat in the chair directly across from the other men. His legs started bouncing under the table. Masking his nervousness proved impossible.

"Derrick, you're one of my deputies, but per Linus' request

I'm putting you on personal leave for you to assist in an assignment."

"Y'all need *me* for an investigation?" He was shocked by the announcement. Trenton was a tight-knit team. They had a few freelancers they pulled in when they needed a stranger's face or backup. Trust was a huge deal for the Trenton team. He was family, but they had a stringent protocol for missions. Hadn't he asked Hunter why they hadn't offered him a job?

"It's a sensitive situation." Hunter didn't say anything else.

He observed Linus as the rough man pushed his chair backward and stood.

"Pure, open the file on the screen."

A pretty, blonde girl, maybe early teens flashed on the flat screen. Her stats scrolled along the right side. She looked a lot younger than her fourteen years. As far as he knew, they never took on missing person or runaway cases. It may sound insensitive, but there wasn't enough action in those situations. Trenton Crew liked to tear shit up too much.

"Almost two weeks ago, Alex Quintin's daughter Cameron disappeared while on vacation with friends. The people she was with turned away for ten minutes, and she was gone. They assumed just typical teenager bullshit, and she'd show up later... that wasn't the case. Dinner time came, and when she still hadn't reappeared, they called Alex and his ex-girlfriend, Margo."

"Does she have a history of running away?" he asked.

"Not once. On the surface, she's a normal teenager. Honor roll. Advanced classes. No boyfriend or girlfriend. So, when she disappeared, it should've been a red flag. I would've taken out the parents that let her get taken."

Linus didn't even change expressions. He knew if something happened to Pride on someone else's watch they'd never find the bodies.

"Gage and Alex have been following leads on their end while we've been working the electronic trail from ours. We've had eyes and ears in just about every auction up and down the east coast," Hunter said.

He didn't know Alex well, but he'd heard the man was a hell of a man to have at your six. He only knew of two occasions Alex had helped the Trenton Crew. After each one, they'd spoken highly of the man. He couldn't imagine what Alex was going through, and he knew Gage was Alex's best friend, which meant that Gage probably considered Cameron a niece.

"Do you need me to help investigate?"

He didn't like how everyone's gaze was suddenly fixed on him.

"In three days time, Gage is going to enter a private estate in the middle of nowhere. We have information that we strongly believe proves that Cameron will be at the location or someone from the party can lead us to her."

Linus and them weren't telling him something, and he didn't like it. That tightening in his gut that always said something bad was coming made him nauseous. He knew the statistics. They were more likely to find her body than to discover her alive after weeks.

"Derrick," Pelter said his name, and he turned his attention to the big man. "We've discussed every option, and while we assumed we'd send Pure in undercover, Pure isn't suitable for the job."

Pelter was an odd addition to the Trenton Crew. It was almost as if Pelter was a freelancer. He found it all odd with Pelter's law and order philosophy. Then he realized he was the second choice and darted his gaze to Pure to find the big man staring at him with an apology in his expressive eyes.

"I'm sorry. If I knew I wouldn't get Gage killed in there I'd do it, but what was being asked of me...I'm sorry."

"What do I need to do?"

"You go in as Gage's boy. His property. I don't like it, and I fought like hell, but we have no one else." Linus' rage was clear in the man's voice.

He darted a panicked look at Hunter, and he knew his dad was no happier with the decision than Linus. A protest was on the tip of his tongue because how the hell could he be in close proximity and not let his personal feelings get in the way.

He could do the job, he had no doubts about his abilities, but could he survive letting the man he loved touch him and not let it affect him?

"With a shave and messy hair, you could still pass for your late teens, early twenties, you're lean. You'd fit the profile. Easily mingle among the others. Gage isn't going to like it. We still haven't informed him that Pure won't be the one inside. Raul was supposed to act as a bodyguard, in this capacity Pure and Raul will be there to watch yours and Gage's backs. While you're inside, what Gage says goes, you don't question. Either of you fucks up, and neither of you makes it out."

Linus was clenching and relaxing his fists at regular intervals. Linus never wanted him to be a cop. Told him repeatedly to find a nice cushy office job. Said he didn't want his son's life to depend on the strength of a vest or that a shooter's aim wasn't true enough to put one between his eyes. He could take the danger. While he wasn't trained as an undercover, he knew how to run an investigation. Except this wasn't some by the book operation. He'd only have Gage and the Trenton team because Pelter wouldn't be able to help. With him gone, the department would be a deputy short on an already small force.

Honesty was best, and he couldn't live if he was at fault for someone's death. "I'm…I don't know if I can be helpful."

"It's a weekend, three days, less if we can get the information we need. All you need to do is follow all of Gage's commands. If he says kneel, you fucking kneel." Linus' every word was an enraged hiss between clenched teeth.

He didn't like the unnaturally quiet men. If he was sure of

anything in life, the Trenton Crew didn't know fuck about keeping their mouths shut. To him that proved this operation wasn't just a simple job—a paycheck—this was about family. Before they'd adopted him, he hadn't understood the concept of being part of something like a family unit.

Did he want someone else watching Gage? He'd worried about Gage since the man went missing. The unknown would be torturous. At least with him working as Gage's partner, he'd know how the man was. He knew he wouldn't be a welcomed surprise for Gage, but as apprehensive as he was about his suitability for assignment, he couldn't say no. He could help find Cameron. He'd deal with the backlash later.

"I'll do it."

Hunter stood and rushed into Linus' open arms. Pelter tossed him a file with all the information they had so far. Pure and Raul outlined the plan and assured him all of that would probably change once they were on the ground. The operation was Gage's show. He was told what to pack by the list Gage sent to Pure. He read through it, and it appeared he wouldn't be wearing clothes very much while he was acting as Gage's boy.

The day at the diner came back to him, and he realized that he'd learn soon what Gage had described. He was suddenly terrified about what lines his brain and body would cross, and if he'd ever be the same when the operation ended.

GAGE WOULD KILL THEM ALL LATER

*H*unter had called to tell them that they'd procured an invite. Hunter was a genius and gave him an identity above reproach with enough truth to make lying easier. Also, the financial portfolio had made him choke with the number of zeros. Alex would front any money necessary to keep up the ruse. They were packing up their things to get ready to go wheels-up in a few hours. Their team was landing any time now, and Gage wasn't ready.

For years, he'd lived as a civilian, making problems disappear or spinning them with Peaches to keep the Trenton team out of jail. He was still in shape, maybe a bit softer with age, but he hadn't lost his ability to handle himself in a firefight. He had to admit before he'd stepped out of the field with the crew that he was one of the best. Decades of training had prepared him for the type of operation Linus ran.

Although, to find Cameron, he'd have to play out all his fantasies with someone he saw as only a friend. Pure would need patience, but he knew he'd have to push the other man past his fears. He didn't know if he had it in him to be that for his friend. Not only would he need to dominate Pure, but he'd also need to ground the man, too. He didn't feel as if he was ready for that responsibility.

"Gage, you ready?"

Alex asked behind him, and he placed the last of his clothes in his duffel. His fingertips stroked over the velvet of two flat, square boxes. One of them contained a necessity, Pure's comfort, and the other was filled with Gage's dreams and insecurities. He'd stood before the display case, a beautiful platinum chain with an ornate lock and key stood out starkly against the plain black leather. When he returned home, he'd hide the collar away with the other treasures he'd held secret for so long.

His life was filled with mysteries he was unwilling to share. His mother's voice filled his head. As if she were close enough for him to scent her perfume she'd only worn on special occasions— when his father was away.

"Gage, honey, come in here a minute."

"Yes, Mama."

She patted her lap, and he didn't complain, he'd lived for the moments they'd curl up on the couch and talk. When his father was around, contact between Gage and her was forbidden. The man didn't want a pussy for a son.

She combed her fingers through his hair as he rested his head on her shoulder.

"You're becoming a young man, Gage. One day you're going to find someone special, and you have to treat them as a gift. That person deserves for you to be gentle and loving. You don't have to be like him, Gage. Caring for someone doesn't mean you control them or hurt them."

"Gage, are you listening to me?"

He spun to look at Alex and realized he'd forgotten the other man was in the room. He turned back quickly to close his bag.

"Yeah, I'm tired and old."

"You and me both. Hunter called and said that we were meeting the team at the airport, then we'll board the private jet to head north."

"Okay, I'll be done in a minute."

He didn't relax his guard until he knew Alex wouldn't be back. He still remembered his mother's hell. Her whippings for breaking the fucker's rules. The choke chain she wore around the house to remind her whom she belonged. The dotted bruises around her pale neck. The Major had used the excuse of a lifestyle to justify his abuse.

She had tried to warn him, to subtly teach him the proper way to care for a partner and he hadn't realized that until years later.

Years passed since he'd touched another person. Linus had ordered him to take a vacation, and while he was halfway across the world, he'd succumbed to his weakness. In the end, he received more satisfaction from jerking off. The man hadn't felt right, and his discouragement caused him to never try again. After mutual orgasms, he sent the man on his way and promised never to repeat.

"Gage, our car is waiting downstairs."

He didn't answer, just slung the straps of his bag over his shoulder and headed for the door. They had so little time to prepare, and he'd only have part of the team with him. He and the Crew functioned better as a single unit. Alex and him spoke sparingly as they were lost in their thoughts. They exited the lobby and let the driver take their bags as they slid into the backseat.

He focused his attention on the scenery outside the window as it shifted from towering buildings to the beach in the distance. The thirty minutes to the airport crept by, and as they pulled up in front of the terminal, he tensed. No way in fuck would they do that—a beautiful boy with dirty blond hair stood flanked by Pure and Raul. The sexy scruff no longer on Derrick's face made him appear younger.

"What the fuck was Linus thinking?" He growled the question. Didn't they understand what would happen to Derrick when the boy was completely at his mercy? He'd have to touch Derrick, maybe more depending on the surveillance around the estate. "I can't do this."

"Gage, he's just a man, a pretty one, but just a man. It's an assignment."

"It's not *just* an assignment or some man. How do I fight my instincts?"

"It's him? The perfect one. The ghost that drifts through your dreams. The one you cut to forget?"

"Has the one person you've dreamed of for years ever appeared? Six years ago, I thought I was fine and"—he turned his attention to Derrick and studied the young man through the tinted glass—"he gave me this sweet, shy smile and I wanted to own him. I can't have him just for that."

"You're not your old man, Gage. The Major is an evil bastard, and he can't be satisfied unless he hurts someone. He gives sadists a bad name. He's reaping his reward, wasting away alone in a nursing home, and no one is going to mourn when he's dead."

On a night with too much drink, he'd told Alex everything, and if Alex hadn't mentioned it the next day, he'd never have remembered his loose tongue.

"Gage, he's just a man. Focus on the mission, the end game and nothing more. Draw the line and don't dare fucking cross it. This is about finding Cameron and bringing her home safe."

He nodded but knew his agreement was a lie. He'd already crossed a line without knowing it. The proof was in his bag, his weakness tangible as the cool metal nestled in a bed of silk. He drew his disinterest and coldness around him, fixed his expression so as not to reveal his true feelings. As him and Alex got out of the car, they took their bags and entered the terminal without sparing the three other men a glance.

They made their way to Alex's jet, and he played a damn good game until they were locked inside, the pilot getting ready to take off. Derrick hadn't looked at him once. Pure and Raul kept their heads down. They both knew they'd fucked up and Derrick wasn't on the team—the boy didn't understand the danger that Gage represented.

He knew Alex had an office set up in the back of the plane. He moved until he stood in front of Derrick. "Stand."

"What…why?"

"Boy, you don't question, you don't hesitate, when I order, you do. Stand."

Derrick shook as he got to his feet. He lifted his left hand to fist his fingers in Derrick's hair winching his head back.

"Gage, don't be a—"

"Raul, you brought the boy here knowing what would happen. He needs to know the game before he gets every one of us fucking killed."

Pure's face was red with rage, but the young man didn't say a word. Pure would fight out of a corner by whatever means necessary, so the man wouldn't have made it a few hours as someone's boy. He knew what Pure thought of Livingston and Fielding, thought being someone's boy was nothing more than degradation. Pure would never trust enough to let someone else care for him.

Derrick's gaze was locked on his chin, and without thinking about the consequences, he forced the boy into Alex's office and locked the door.

"Strip," he barked out the order. "No, you don't argue, if I tell you to get naked and kneel at my feet, you will do so without complaint. If you're not convincing, we lose whatever traction we have. Now, fucking strip."

The rage he always kept under control surged to the surface

to mask what he felt. He didn't like ravaging the boy. With his arms crossed over his chest, he straightened his spine and watched Derrick strip, first kicking off his boots. His increased respiration had nothing to do with his anger as smooth tanned skin stretched over lean muscle was slowly exposed. The same pink blush that stained Derrick's pretty face the day he'd told him his boy's place would be on his knees for him highlighted strong cheekbones. His chest was hairless with flat pectorals. Derrick's stomach wasn't defined, just soft skin with an outie bellybutton.

He felt like a bastard when his cock started to harden at the short pause as Derrick dropped his jeans and pink briefs to pool around his ankles. Derrick covered his slender, average-sized length with both hands.

"Did you come here thinking I'd play with you? Make those silly fantasies of yours come true?"

"N—no, they asked me, and I thought I could, I just wanted to help."

"Once we enter that estate, it's just the two of us. One moment of hesitation…" He paused and approached Derrick as he dropped his arms. He steeled himself for the first touch. "And we draw attention. You don't question. You have no choice but to trust me without question. I'll touch you when and how I want." He circled behind Derrick and stroked his fingertips down the indent of Derrick's spine to the top of his crease. Derrick's cheeks were rounded with the cutest dimples. "You have to trust me above all others, and when I say something, don't question. If my ownership is mistrusted—" He didn't want to finish the sentence. Instead, he pressed to Derrick's back. The boy fit perfectly against him, and he inhaled the boy's scent. "You're mine for the duration of this operation. Do you trust me?" He lowered his head and brushed his lips to the slender strength of Derrick's shoulder.

"Yes."

Derrick's soft voice was breathy, and he leaned into Gage.

"No hesitation, and if we have to play, you play. But I'll make one thing clear...it means nothing, am I understood?" He pretended to be satisfied with the slight nod, and he quickly moved away. "Get dressed and in your seat, we'll talk more when we land and get to the hotel. By the time we start this operation, you'll be ready because if you're not, my niece might be lost forever if she isn't already."

He ignored the boy's flinch and left the office, and then he took his seat before buckling in. He grabbed his laptop to check his emails and to see if Hunter sent him any more information. Linus had also earned an email about the Derrick bullshit. Derrick shouldn't be anywhere near this operation, but the damaged part of him wanted to be selfish. All he wanted was a night to learn what Derrick sounded like in his pleasure and to memorize the bliss that he knew only he could give Derrick. But he also knew that it couldn't be, and he needed to remember that it was all an act—Derrick would never belong to him.

DERRICK SHOULD'VE SAID NO

*H*e'd never stayed in a room as nice as the bedroom they'd given him when they'd checked into the suite. In a few hours, they'd leave for the estate. For almost two days, Gage had ruthlessly worked to destroy any urge he had to resist —to question—and he had to remember it was all a show. That was harder to remember when Gage appeared almost loving, and it reminded him of the way Livingston took care of Fielding. Making sure he was happy and safe, and he'd lost count of the times Gage had pulled him down on his lap just to hold him.

The discomfort had lessened, but the disapproving looks from the other three men had made him self-conscious. It made him wonder how many messages and updates his dads were getting. The day before Gage had ordered him to strip in front of them all. He'd fought back the tears as the arguments raged around him. In the end, Gage had won, outlining every detail of what he'd probably see. How was he supposed to ignore what was going on around him and never speak up?

His role fit like a cheap, too small suit, but his mind played it through his head in detail. Gage hadn't spared him any details.

The profile and intel they had on their host showed a man who had more money than morality, and he didn't want to think about what that meant for the people they allegedly bought. His gut told him something wasn't right, but he couldn't put his finger on what that was, and his frustration grew. It was all too easy.

Gage's actions confused him, one minute he played the loving Daddy to perfection and the next his pride was shredded as the man berated him. He was informed that he'd have to adapt. Slave or boy, an object or a treasure.

He was enjoying some privacy while he had it. Gage had warned him once they entered the gates, they'd be under surveillance twenty-four, seven. Hunter had tapped into the security system, and cameras were placed in every room. He opened his laptop, signed in and opened the encrypted messaging app Hunter wrote the code for.

"I'll send you a ticket."

He chuckled as he watched his dad twist his long hair into a loose bun. The dark circles were noticeable beneath Hunter's eyes. Every video call Hunter seemed more exhausted and aged beyond his years.

"Dad, I'll be fine."

"We shouldn't have put you in this. It's too fucking much."

Hunter appeared as if he hadn't slept in days and he had a feeling the man wouldn't sleep right until he returned home. Hunter had become overprotective the moment they'd met. They hadn't known what a family was supposed to be until the three of them. All the times he'd dreamed of what parents would be, he hadn't fully understood until Hunter and his husbands made them their sons.

"It's a few days. I'll be fine."

"Linus isn't happy with how Gage is treating you."

What had they expected when they sent him undercover? Pure always seemed as if he wasn't afraid of anything. The thought of being under someone else's control terrified Pure. If anyone other than Gage was going in with him, he didn't believe he'd have agreed. His agreement while he wanted to help—to save the girl—it was also selfish, a moment to spend with Gage.

"Would he be happier if it was Pure?"

"Pure isn't our kid."

"But he's one of the team…family. I'll be fine. I promise."

"I know you're an adult. Were before you even came to us, but that doesn't change that I love you like a son."

"They need me to find Cameron, and I can do that. When I get home, everything will be normal or as normal as it gets around there."

He felt better when Hunter smiled, but he rolled his eyes as Linus appeared on the screen. His arms wrapped around Hunter's neck and the kiss Linus placed on Hunter's cheek was sweet. The love between his three dads was something he aspired to have one day.

"I can kill him."

"Pop, I have no doubt, but it isn't necessary."

He attempted to hide his smile as Hunter turned his head to press his face into the side of Linus' neck. It was an action he'd seen Wren and Hunter make a thousand times over the years. For them, it was as natural as breathing to seek comfort in the same way.

"I think it's very fucking necessary."

"You just want to kill something…you're getting soft in your old age." Surprisingly, Linus had mellowed over the years, but that didn't mean he didn't welcome some bloodshed every now and again.

"I'll kick your ass when you get home for that."

"I love y'all, too."

"Derrick, one word, one signal and you're out, we'll be watching," Hunter assured him.

He cringed at the possibility. "Please don't watch."

"Okay, we won't be watching, but Raul and Pure have orders to get you out by any means. We'll hide the bodies." If anything was a certainty when it came to Linus, it was that the man was homicidal on a good day.

"You do pay Peaches an obscene retainer."

"She needs to earn it. Can't just have her looking pretty around the office. I'm going to take my gorgeous husbands out to dinner. Pride is spending the night with Sawyer and Ricky."

Linus made life seem so simple, and he'd always owe them a debt for the life they'd given Pride. He couldn't imagine his baby brother as he would've turned out with their biological parents. Pride was a million times better than he would've been growing up with Thorpe and their mother.

"Take advantage of that kid-free house."

They said their goodbyes and made plans, well, he was given orders before the screen went blank, then he closed the lid, and stowed his laptop in his backpack. A knock preceded the door opening, and he looked up as Gage walked in. He tensed as Gage closed them in the room. The big man was dressed in a long-sleeved t-shirt and worn jeans. Gage's hair was messy as if he'd run his fingers through it constantly.

"You ready?"

"I'd lie and say yes, but I think you'd know."

"It's seventy-two hours. We should be good for that amount of time."

There was a question he wanted to ask but hadn't wanted to do that in front of Alex. "Gage, may I ask something?"

He shoved his bag aside as Gage took a seat on the bed. He noticed the flat box Gage set between them.

"This doesn't work if we're not open and trust in each other."

"What if we don't find her? I didn't want to ask with Alex around."

"I don't know. We've checked with every one of our contacts. Livingston is chasing every Jane Doe reported. Little and Hunter are looking through every second of security tape on international flights.

"I was there the night Cameron was born. I broke quite a few laws to make sure Alex made it stateside to be there. She was the most beautiful, tiniest thing I'd ever seen. I love her, but I can't possibly understand what Alex and Margo are going through."

"Why isn't Margo here?"

"She's working every angle. She arrived at Trenton Security a few hours after we left. She's driving Livingston insane."

"I just don't want to fu—" He almost rolled his eyes as Gage raised one thick brow. "Screw, screw up."

"Good boy, you'll do great. If all else fails, just follow my lead. We do have one thing to take care of before we leave."

"What?"

"When we arrive, you have to wear something that shows who you belong to. As long as you wear it"—Gage picked up the box and lifted the top off—"you're off limits. It's the only protection I can offer."

He stared down at the beautiful length of chain, the two ends secured by a lock with ornate scrollwork. It appeared to be a lock that would grace a treasure chest. Nestled beside it was an old-fashioned key on a thinner chain. Fielding wore a ring crafted to be a delicate length of chain. Sin and Saint, Pelter's husbands had tattoos that matched the one that Pelter had. These were to show ownership, an agreement as binding as wedding vows. His heart broke as he stared at the collar.

"If something happens, you're to find Raul and Pure. They'll get you to safety. You save yourself, do you understand?"

He wanted to protest. He wasn't useless. And wasn't it the Trenton policy to never leave anyone behind? For days Gage had threatened to put him over his knee, and as much fun as he'd once assumed that would be, he wasn't in the mood for his first punishment yet.

"Yes."

Gage had removed the chain and was running the length through his fingers. He held his breath as Gage leaned in closer and looped it around his neck. His eyes fell shut to conceal his pain with the quiet click of the lock. He peeked from under his lashes and was fascinated by Gage's expression. It was almost unreadable, but the lack of emotion piqued his curiosity. Gage might play his hand close to the vest, but Gage was never completely emotionless. His eyes always gave him away. Gage kept staring at it as he fingered the lock and the back of the man's fingers stroked his skin through his t-shirt.

The heaviness of the chain seemed as if it weighed him down and he wished it meant more than three days of protection. For almost a decade, he'd dreamed of growing up and belonging to Gage, proving himself worthy of the standoffish man's love and affection. He barely suppressed the urge to grab the man's hand as Gage retreated and lifted the other chain—the man's big hands awkward as they tried to release the clasp.

"Want me to do it?"

Gage nodded as he handed over the chain with the key, the decorations matched the lock. He used his nail to open it, and he leaned forward, his arms around Gage's neck. The big man's face was close enough to his that he felt the warm rush of breath across his cheek.

He straightened to put a safe distance between them. "It's beautiful, you shouldn't have, a plain one would've been fine," he said as he raised his hand to trace the links under his fingertips. It was slowly warming where it rested on his skin.

"A beautiful collar for a beautiful boy," Gage said in a tone barely above a whisper. "Get a couple of hours of rest, and I'll wake you in time to get ready before we leave."

Gage didn't waste time escaping, and he disappeared through the door before he had time to respond. He was too nervous to sleep. His emotions were in knots, tangled in the uncertainty of what could've been and the darkness of reality. For seventy-two hours, he'd belong to Gage, but when their time was up, he'd move on with his life. The older man wasn't meant to be his. Yet, he'd always remember the man he loved calling him beautiful.

WHAT HAD GAGE BEEN THINKING?

The suit Gage wore was perfectly tailored and highlighted the broadness of his shoulders while concealing the slight curve of his belly. The wave of his silver hair tamed enough that he looked presentable. He sat in the back of the limo their host had sent for them. Derrick was seated across from him between Pure and Raul. They looked out of place in their own suits while Derrick looked comfortable in slacks and a button-down shirt. The top two buttons were undone to expose the collar.

He'd stood beside his bed that afternoon staring down at the two boxes. The length of plain leather was supposed to be the one that graced Derrick's neck, but when it had come time for him to choose, there was only one choice. What the fuck had he thought when he'd secured the chain around Derrick's throat? He'd imagined his boy wearing nothing except the chain while Derrick was in his bed.

He'd bought the leather collar with Pure in mind, but the one Derrick currently wore was purchased for his boy. His attraction could no longer be ignored. He just couldn't give in to what he'd dreamed of since his boy's college graduation. He imagined all the ways he'd take care of his boy. How he would make sure Derrick never wanted for anything. Claiming him would be easy, isn't that what he'd always wanted?

Just let him go. And hadn't he given Liv the same advice? What happened if the monster the Major created burst forth and he hurt Derrick? He couldn't allow that to happen. Livingston had believed himself incapable of love and wanted a better life for Fielding, but in the end—he shook his head and adjusted the cuffs of his linen shirt. His watch and a leather cuff concealing the scars which might peek from under the fabric. Those lines in different degrees of recovery showed as proof of why, in three days time, he had to let Derrick go.

His ritual of cutting each morning was weeks overdue. Alex knew of them and hiding the evidence was useless, but new bandages would've had Alex on his ass.

The vehicle pulled to a stop outside a towering iron gate. Gage instantly took inventory, and the guard at the gate didn't appear to be holding anything other than a clipboard. The house beyond the fence was three stories that screamed obscene wealth, and he briefly made eye contact with Pure and Raul. After the driver and the guard exchanged a few words, the gate started to open with the grinding of metal against metal.

They'd reached the point of no return. Once inside, they were on their own. Alex would set up at a safe distance and await the rest of the team's arrival later that night. He'd hoped to have them stay in Powers and away from the action, not because he didn't need them, but because he just wanted to protect Derrick. While most of what happened inside had to appear to be nothing more than a role, once he'd had his hands on Derrick, it had turned into more.

He'd relished the so-called lessons, and when Derrick's weight was on his lap, he'd barely resisted pressing his lips to his boy's ear to whisper his intention to keep him. That couldn't be though. He felt like a fraud, and he couldn't let Derrick into his head.

They made the short trip around the circular drive, and the large front door opened. As a man in a tux opened the car door, all his attention was on the man that stepped onto the porch. He appeared to be a few years older than himself. Cultured and perfect. He slipped out of the back, and as he straightened, he buttoned his suit jacket. He took two steps forward to allow the other men out.

"Mr. Gage, it is a pleasure to make your acquaintance. I'm Maurice Forester."

He schooled his features as he moved forward and accepted the man's extended hand. Forester had the look of a man who had everything handed to him.

"Please, call me, Hayden. I was surprised that I was invited to attend. You have a very exclusive club."

"We just have similar tastes, and fresh blood is rare."

Forester looked past him, and he nearly growled at the interest that bloomed in the man's cold blue eyes. He pivoted on his toes to find Derrick's gaze trained on the ground and his boy was playing with the lock where it rested between Derrick's collarbones.

"I was unaware you'd be bringing your own entertainment and security with you."

"My boy goes everywhere with me along with his personal security. I pay them exceptionally well to protect what's mine."

"We are a group with rules. Unless you expressly share your toy...he will be off-limits. It would be a shame not to be gifted with a sample."

Derrick barely suppressed a jerk at Forester's mention of having a sample, and he hated that those words affected his boy so strongly. Sharing wouldn't happen. If someone even looked as if they were going to touch his boy, they'd realize he wasn't as cultured as he looked. "My boy and I have an agreement. He's signed himself over to me. I own everything, especially his pleasure and I'm not a generous man."

"Very well. We have readied a room for you. You're one of the first to arrive. My other guests embrace a rather fashionably late philosophy. I'll have my assistant Saler find your security a room. Would you prefer one close to you or will any room do?"

"Any room should be fine. My boy doesn't need them when I'm around, but they are to be at his beck and call."

"Very well. Dinner is at nine, and then we'll have a meeting to discuss the rules of our event. Please, until then make yourselves at home."

He couldn't resist studying what he could see of the house—mentally calculating escape routes. Raul and Pure would stake out the house later under the guise of their roles as Derrick's security. They were shown to the second floor to an extravagantly decorated bedroom. The driver placed his and Derrick's suitcase on the bench at the foot of the bed, his garment bag in the closet and left without a word. Saler asked if there was anything they needed and when he replied no, Saler led Pure and Raul from the room. He could see their reluctance to leave, but he needed time alone with Derrick before dinner.

His boy stood completely still in the middle of the room, and as Derrick was told, he remained still waiting for orders. He removed his suit jacket and strode to the closet to hang it on velvet covered hangers. When he would normally roll up his sleeves, he refrained. The weight of his secrets exhausted him more every day.

"Strip," he ordered without turning around.

When he glanced over his shoulder, he noticed Derrick hadn't moved. He rushed across the room and wrapped his hand around the front of his boy's throat.

"Daddy gave you an order, boy." He didn't even recognize his voice, and he fisted his free hand in the front of Derrick's shirt and tore it, buttons pinged off the hardwood floors. "Drop your pants to your ankles and bend over the bed." He shoved Derrick back and felt like a sick fucker as Derrick obeyed.

Pale, fuzzy cheeks were exposed, and then Derrick bent over —Derrick's hands sinking into the thick covers.

He had no doubt Forester was watching. The man didn't trust him. It was in the too polite smile and friendly demeanor. He was too welcoming for a stranger. While his bank account had probably helped, if what was going on here even came close to what he expected, then he needed to convince the bastard he was who he said he was.

He approached the boy. Derrick was so beautifully masculine. His belly wasn't cut but had just the slightest softness to it. His cheeks were plump. He bent over Derrick. His chest to Derrick's back. "When I say to do something, do it," he whispered.

"I'm sorry."

"Sorry what?"

"I'm sorry, D...Daddy."

"Now you're going to be punished. Don't disobey again."

He straightened in a rush and turned to the side. He curved his hand around Derrick's opposite hip and brought his hand back, he paused only long enough to build anticipation, and then he struck. Derrick's cheeks jiggled under the force. "You will receive twelve. You will count them for me and thank me for each one, is that understood? Start at two, boy."

Each time his hand met his boy's...his—he needed to remember that Derrick wasn't his—but it was so hard to do as his boy counted and thanked Daddy for punishment. His body didn't want to pretend, and each strike was harder than the last. His pale ass was red and blooming with perfect welted handprints. He could sense Derrick wanted to fight, to move away from the pain, but every yelp was music to his ears. He noticed the change in Derrick's breathing and the subtle lift of his boy's hips.

He gave Derrick the last one then sat down on the bed. His boy's beautiful eyes were half-mast, and he pulled Derrick into his lap. The trembling of Derrick's body and the way his boy melted into him was heaven and hell. He kissed Derrick's forehead as he soothed his boy. He enjoyed the panting breaths against his chest. "My beautiful boy, you have to listen to me. I only do it to help you learn. You could get hurt if you don't obey."

"Yes, Daddy, I'm sorry."

If there were mics in the room, the words were spoken too low to be picked up. The lines were already blurred. Gage had imagined this for too many years. Derrick was always the one he jerked his cock to at night. Fantasized about the blissed-out look, but when he was alone once again, he'd know his boy's ecstasy. Derrick seemed to go limp, and his breathing evened out. He didn't control his urge to smile as he stood to gently lay his boy on the bed. He was too restless to sleep or join Derrick on the big bed.

He stripped Derrick of the ruined shirt, his shoes and socks, until his boy wore nothing except the collar. He grabbed the soft blanket at the foot of the bed and shook it out before laying it over his sleeping boy. Derrick mumbled in his sleep, and he left him to prepare for the evening. When he exited the bedroom, an enraged Pure was staring at him, and Raul just looked amused.

"I'm going for a walk. My boy is napping. No one gets in, am I understood?"

"Yes, sir. He'll be safe and sound." Pure's answer was pushed through clenched teeth.

He nodded and headed for the stairs to make a loop of the house. If he wasn't mistaken, him and Pure were going to have issues after this operation was over. That wasn't much of a surprise. Pure could joke as much as the rest of them, but sex wasn't something the other man ever spoke lightly about. Everyone assumed Pure just waited for when he met someone worthy, but he'd always thought it was more than that. There was something haunted in the big man's gaze. He'd been shocked when no one pried because that's what the Trenton team did best. Secrets weren't something they tolerated.

"Hayden, I thought you'd be resting."

He turned to find Forester typing away on his phone, and he wondered if every camera was linked to the device.

"I'm a restless man."

"Please have a seat." Forester motioned to the chair across from him. "Your background check showed you were in the military."

He took the seat offered and tried to appear relaxed. "I enlisted in the Navy right out of high school. It wasn't my calling, but I wanted out of Texas." He was thankful Hunter used as much of his real information as possible, and the Navy hadn't been what he'd always wanted to do, but it had been his way out.

"Very noble profession. It says you work in Public Relations."

"Yes. I work for a Security company, let's just say they're not very civilized, but they pay exceptionally well. Off the books, I work with private clients to make...situations disappear. I can't speak about them. Trust is a very valuable commodity in what I do."

"Your bank account says you're very well sought after."

"I take pride in what I do. It also allows me to travel quite a bit."

"And your travel companion is rather beautiful. Is your agreement exclusive? I have acquired some exceptional party favors."

"He pledged his loyalty to me, and to be respectful of my boy, I don't play with others. For the time being that works in my favor, I may get him a companion at some point. I'm restless and easily bored, he has yet to bore me. He's still willful enough to make punishing him...interesting."

The quick smile that tilted the man's lips proved that he'd

watched the punishment take place. He wasn't surprised but more pissed off at the man daring to look at his boy.

"I find the punishment more enjoyable, but unlike you, I find variety works best for me. A few of my guests will bring their own entertainment but will also take advantage of what I provide, but I will respect your wishes. We believe very much in consensual play. There's too many who think breaking their toys is the point. I find them barbaric."

Shit, if that were true, then he wouldn't find Cameron there. Safe and consensual had nothing to do with the people who probably purchased his niece. Although, the man could speak all the pretty words he wanted, they'd know more later.

"I'm being informed my guests are beginning to arrive, would you like to greet them with me? Maybe become familiar before tonight's festivities."

He agreed but was in no mood to socialize. He hadn't made it around to check the place out as he'd wanted. He'd prefer to know every path of escape especially since he'd left his weapon in the hotel suite. They'd discussed that it wouldn't look good to be armed. That in no way meant that they were any less dangerous. They all excelled at hand to hand, close quarter combat. He stood and followed the other man to the front entrance. Limos started to line up to drop off passengers. Most were alone, but a few had guards. He recognized some faces from the news. These men were the who's who of the rich and famous.

The last limo stopped at the base of the steps and the man who stepped out set him instantly on edge. It didn't get much better when a boy who looked far too young and nothing but skin and bones exited. The collar around his neck had chaffed the skin raw. This was a broken boy—nothing more than a shell with no spirit left. He made a note to speak with Raul and Pure to have them keep an eye on the man.

"Francois, what a pleasure you could join us again."

He glanced from the corner of his eye and noticed his host

voice was tighter, not as polite. The bastard's expression wasn't much friendlier, and he wondered why the man received an invite when it appeared Forester and the other man weren't friends. He was impatient to return to his room to speak with his team. If this was a dead end in finding Cameron, at least he could save someone.

WHAT THE FUCK HAD DERRICK BEEN THINKING?

$\mathcal{D}$errick peered in the mirror and didn't recognize himself. He'd thought Gage had prepared him for what would happen when they started the mission. Everything had changed the moment Gage's rough hand wrapped around his throat. He was horrified at how his cock had hardened as the pain of his punishment had morphed into something else. The agony had bordered on pleasure, and then at the fifth strike, he felt the first drop of precum on his thigh. He had no longer played his role, and as Gage had pressed his cock to his ass, his shame bloomed hotter at the lack of response on the other man's part.

He'd hidden his tears as Gage had positioned him on his lap. He hadn't meant to fall asleep, but he'd felt exhausted. He hadn't awakened until Gage had returned. When Gage had stretched out beside him, he hadn't hesitated to curl against the bigger man's side. They'd spoken in whispers and pretended they weren't discussing a new development. Gage wanted him to keep an eye on a boy who'd arrived with one of the other guests.

"We're due at dinner," Gage called through the door.

"Yes, Daddy, I'm coming." That title for Gage flowed too easily off his tongue. He realized that when they returned home after finding Cameron things would return to normal for Gage. Him, not so much.

He exited the bathroom wearing an identical outfit to the one he arrived in and was thankful. He found being naked around Gage okay, but not altogether comfortable, so he didn't think he'd handle it around strangers. As much as the act was fake in his heart, he had always belonged to Gage. As much as he wanted to tense, he remained relaxed as Gage approached him and undid another button to expose the collar.

"Boy, your collar is to remain exposed at all times."

The door opened behind Gage, and he smiled at Pure and Raul. Without a word, they took their places on either side of him. He took comfort in their protection. It was decided that no one would touch him other than Gage. Same as earlier, Gage took point, and the other two men watched his six. They made their way downstairs silently into the massive dining room. Men lined the table, and it was easy enough to find the boy he was supposed to watch.

He doubted the boy was more than eighteen wearing nothing more than leather pants and a collar. It wasn't like his, but thick and black with a large ring—a leash attached to it. He was painfully thin with sunken cheeks and eyes. The boy was kneeling behind the man's chair with his back to the seat. He wanted to tell the boy to get up.

He was surprised when he was offered the chair beside Gage, and Pure and Raul placed themselves in the shadows not far behind where they sat. He kept his gaze on the table.

"Welcome, it appears everyone is here. I'd like to introduce the newest member of our group. Hayden Gage. He brought his own boy, so please respect his ownership. Another season has passed, and it is an honor to be among you all again. Please, enjoy dinner, and we'll retire to the study and let the games begin."

He ignored most of the conversation, and he reached for nothing as men in tuxedos moved around placing plates. He jerked as he was completely skipped, then the plate with the bowl of soup on it that had been placed in front of Gage was moved in front of him, then wine filled his glass to the halfway point. Gage tenderly stroked his cheek.

"Eat, boy."

"Yes, Daddy." He was too nervous to eat. He felt eyes on him, and he was too aware of the young man who wasn't being fed. He swore he heard the boy's stomach growl. Just as he was about to open his mouth and ask if he could give his food to the boy, the server returned and placed a new plate in front of Gage.

The meal was one of those fancy ones with course after course. He followed Gage's lead when it came to what spoons and forks to use. Each bite he took made him feel guilty as the ignored boy was offered none. The discussions around him went right over his head. It was all business and profit, investors and board of directors. This could've been any dinner shared by businessmen and not a meal before the men played with whomever the host offered. Toys to be used and it all seemed sickeningly civilized.

He had no issues with kink or BDSM, but it wasn't his scene. The few times he'd had sex in the past was all rather vanilla. Two people getting off, going through the motions, well, he'd gone through the motions. He understood it wasn't cheating. Except it wasn't Gage, so it never felt quite right. His obsession became his secret shame. What would happen when he went back to his real life? Putting on his uniform, the weight of Gage's ownership no longer around his neck, and his love unrequited.

The food no longer had a taste, but he forced each bite as not to draw attention. By the time dessert was served, he was barely keeping what he ate down. His nervousness tore at his stomach as he pictured what was to come next. Would Gage spank him and show off for the other men? He wasn't an exhibitionist. What happened between two people was private, and he didn't want witnesses to how weak he was to resist, how quickly he gave in.

It hadn't passed his notice that occasionally Gage would offer him bites off his plate or held the wineglass to his lips. Every time he glanced at Gage there was something off and intense about the look in his eyes. No one had ever studied him as deeply as the older man had done. When he took the offerings, Gage praised him and stroked his cheek. There was one thing Gage hadn't done in the days leading up to the operation and since they arrived, Gage hadn't kissed him. The man would brush kisses to his forehead, sometimes his shoulder when Gage came up behind him, but never his mouth.

How pathetic was he that he wanted one kiss before all this ended?

So lost in his thoughts, he was surprised when it was announced everyone was to head to the study to continue their evening. His legs shook as he stood.

"Please instruct your security to remain outside the room," Forester announced.

While he felt safer with his friends there, he was strangely relieved that they wouldn't witness what was going to happen. He knew his dad was tapped into the security system and had access to the cameras. They'd promised not to watch, but someone had to, and he had a feeling another member of the team or Alex was tasked with keeping watch.

He almost protested as the slick looking bastard with the French accent made the boy crawl like a dog. His head at an unnatural angle by how high the fucker held the leash. As soon as he opened his mouth, Gage's hand landed on the small of his back and stroked soothingly across his skin. Gage bent his head to place his mouth right next to his ear.

"I already signaled for Alex to inform Hunter to do some inquiries. He's already part of the rescue."

He nodded in answer because he didn't trust his voice and he bit the inside of his cheek until he tasted blood when the boy was ordered into a corner. His face pressed into it. He waited for Gage to order him to do the same, but Gage pushed him to his knees beside a leather wingback chair, then took a seat. Gage's words came back to him, and he leaned his head on Gage's knee as strong fingers stroked through his hair. It was a soothing caress over his scalp, and he knew Gage was trying to calm him down.

As cruel as it was to put the boy in the corner at least the bastard couldn't touch him anymore. Another man in a tux made the rounds of the chairs in front of a fire and served drinks. Forester stood in front of the fireplace as if ready to give a toast.

"As we have a new guest with us, I feel I must repeat the rules for everyone."

If he wasn't mistaken, Forester's gaze landed on Francois a moment longer than the rest of the men in the room. If he wasn't liked then why did he get an invite?

"I have arranged entertainment for the weekend. As per house rules, you must ask consent in front of a witness to acknowledge that your play this weekend is consensual. A safe word must be established before said scenes. Consent can be taken back at any time. Please respect the safety and wishes of your sub. The breaking of any of these rules will have you escorted off the property and if needed authorities notified. Trust is your greatest reward, do not cheapen it. With that said, enjoy your time here and don't doubt you'll be watched to make sure adherence to all rules and verbal contracts."

He was a pretty good judge of character, and he didn't get the feeling the man was lying. He adhered to safe, sane, and consensual. Did they find the wrong party? Were they wasting precious time? He mentally shook his head, there was someone who needed to be freed, and if he succeeded at nothing else, the boy would be free before they were done. He made sure to keep an eye on the boy while Gage spoke with Forester.

Forester raised his arm and motioned to someone, a door on the opposite side of the room opened, and a group of ten men and women walked in. They wore nothing but white robes, and they all looked over eighteen. There was one for each of the guests and host. He wrapped his arms around Gage's calf.

"As our newest member has his pet with him, I will take advantage of his choice tonight."

"I'm more than happy with that decision. My boy is all I need." A stranger probably wouldn't have noticed the growl in Gage's voice, but he'd studied everything about the man over the last ten years, and he was familiar with the sound of anger in Gage's tone.

Lights came up and took the edges of the room out of darkness. Crosses and benches were placed around the room. Whips, floggers and other toys were in displays along the walls. Everyone except Gage picked one of the choices, and he listened as consent was asked for and given. Some lowered themselves onto large cushions to observe the ones beginning to perform.

Forester returned to take the chair beside Gage, and the man had chosen a beautiful blonde woman.

"I sense your boy's nervousness." Forester motioned to the ground for the woman to kneel.

She almost mirrored his pose, and she secretly smiled at him. When she winked, he returned her grin. He didn't know what he'd assumed this would be, but it came nowhere near the reality. Moans filled the room. Leather, wood or hands meeting flesh echoed in the cavernous space. He couldn't hide his blush.

"This is the first time I've shared his presence with others. We agreed that he would only do as much as he's comfortable doing."

"Janette is mine. I mix her in with the others on these nights. She's very upset about being banished from her home before events."

"Don't they recognize her?" Gage asked.

"They think she's just the one I favor. She has put up with my stubborn, dominant ways for quite a few years now. She was one of the first, and after I met her, she was mine. These men as much as I consider most of them my friends, we rarely mingle outside of these parties. May I address your boy?"

He lifted his head to catch Gage nodding.

"Sex isn't allowed in the main room. If that happens it's a private moment among the couple or group, but never in here. I'm not one to share very well. I don't like my girl to be looked at by other men. These men"—Forester motioned behind him—"they don't care, it's all about the scene and having a bit of fun while away from wives and husbands."

"Then why do it?" Gage sounded confused, and he understood why.

"Tradition. My father did the same, and I carried it on after his death several years ago. Everything is still run in his name. I prefer my privacy. My girl indulges me. There is a lot to be said for familiarity. I rarely participate until the room clears and then I give her what she needs."

"How can you tell if things are getting out of hand?"

"Janette has informed our security staff to monitor activities and report if anything is...unusual."

"Do they know you watch them?" Gage asked.

"It's a fact that isn't discussed beyond a mention like tonight. Everyone is aware they are always being watched. We've had a few incidents over the years of people with ill-intentions."

"You're very open with your set-up here."

He felt Gage tense where he rested his head on the man's thigh and his fingers tense a little too tightly in his hair. Maybe Gage was having the same thoughts as him that they'd been sent on a wild goose chase. That this wasn't a step closer to finding Gage's niece.

"One tradition I won't carry on from my father is his Sadism. He was only interested in hurting, and while I don't shame people for their needs, I won't facilitate torture. Once consent is expressed that's on them, but I won't have men in our home who hurt people just for the sake of hurting them. What they do outside my home is their business."

"What about when it's brought into your home?"

He glanced at Gage to find the man looking at the boy in the corner.

"He treats that boy like a hated pet, but he doesn't lay hands on Kray while here. I think the boy gets a bit of a reprieve and Janette sneaks him food when Francois is busy. We've asked him questions…if he'd like to stay with us, but whatever was done to him has broken his will. He assures us he's eighteen and Francois has provided the contract and ID. If someone is brought into our home, it is the first thing we request."

"You didn't ask me."

"Your boy is well-loved. Healthy. Never ventures from your side. You fed him before you fed yourself. That was a test. I purposely asked him not to be served. We were informed he earned punishment earlier but that it went no further than correction."

His face flamed as he leaned heavier on Gage's leg. Knowing there was a possibility they were being watched to being informed they were added up to two different things. It didn't appear as if they were being forced to participate, and while he was grateful, he was also a bit disappointed. That part of him that loved Gage wanted a few memories to take home with him.

"Don't be embarrassed. They watched no longer than to make sure it wasn't excessive. Janette took great care in choosing them, but I won't lie and say they don't watch occasionally for the fun."

It was all rather surreal that Forester and Gage spoke as friends while surrounded by whippings and scenes playing out. He relaxed realizing, for at least tonight, he wouldn't be put on display in front of others. That didn't apply to their room though. They now knew they were being watched, would they have to pretend to be together? He didn't let his nerves build, he'd worry about all that later. He spoke quietly with Janette while studying the lone boy across the room. There had to be something they could do, and he'd ask tonight while they were alone and hidden by darkness.

GAGE WAS A SICK FUCK

*T*he pressure of the scalding hot water hit the back of his neck and down his back. Derrick had already had his shower and was curled up in bed. He needed a moment to himself to get his thoughts straight. His privacy was important to him and being around people twenty-four-seven was starting to take its toll on his nerves. He admitted to himself that the night was enlightening and altogether too disappointing. After enjoying a conversation with Forester and studying the scenes playing out around them, he doubted this man had bought Cameron. Also, a new operation had popped up, rescue the boy Francois was obviously abusing. He'd met quite a few masochists in his day, they savored the pain and marks left, but that wasn't the boy. When Pure and Raul had escorted them back to the room, he'd relayed what he knew and mentioned Francois and Kray. It would be easy enough to run a search for missing kids. Kray was an unusual name.

His team promised they'd get the information out to Alex, but he'd sworn them to secrecy about his fear that he wouldn't find Cameron there. If he knew his best friend, the man was already tearing himself up over whether Cameron was alive or not. He was already having the same thoughts. Even if she was still breathing, the more days that passed, the less likely they'd find her.

He'd thought about children over the years, when his friends were having babies or adopting. A family was never in his plans and still wasn't, but that didn't stop him from thinking about the bond between his friends and their partners. He'd wondered if his life had been different would he have had a husband. Yet, when those thoughts began to form, he always pushed them away. His loneliness was something he'd grown used to, and in his late forties, his time had passed him by.

Exhaustion weighed him down, so he finished washing himself with quick, efficient movements. He turned off the water and stepped out of the large glass stall. Pajama bottoms were the only thing he'd brought with him to wear after his shower. He'd made sure the lights were low, and unless Derrick looked too closely, the boy wouldn't notice the scars. As he dried his chest, he wiped the fog from the mirror and looked at himself.

He wasn't one to study his reflection. His body was hairy and still in pretty good shape. At his age and with his job, the middle-aged spread wasn't surprising. He wondered what Derrick saw in him. He wasn't clueless, the boy wanted him, and unfortunately, the feeling was mutual. The operation needed to end soon. It was becoming harder to resist the lure of the younger man. Derrick wasn't hardened enough to hide his reaction. The spanking earlier had shown him quite clearly that his boy was perfect for him.

None of that could be, though. Gage finished up and hung his towel up to dry. He stepped into his sleep pants. The soft cotton waistband rested just on his hips below the slight curve of his stomach. He should put on underwear since he was going to be in the same bed as Derrick. That lean body nestled into the curve of his, fuck, he was already wondering what Derrick's soft ass would feel like against his cock.

They were going to have to be close together so they'd have a chance to talk privately. He had no doubt that whoever was manning the cameras would watch their every move. His thin pants would be no protection for either of them. Then a thought hit him, what would Derrick's lips feel like under his. He'd avoided that one intimacy.

He opened the bathroom door and turned off the light, the sconces on the wall were dimmed enough that most of the room was in shadow. It only highlighted Derrick's form in the bed. The boy curled on his side, hugging the pillow to his chest. What he planned was dangerous, but he was also a selfish man. He stopped beside the bed and lifted the covers to slip beneath them. He stretched out behind Derrick, slipped his arm beneath Derrick's head and roughly tugged the boy completely against him with his hand that was rested on Derrick's belly.

A groan threatened to escape, and he barely caught it before it had a chance to alert Derrick to the torture of being so close. He'd never slept beside someone before. Sex for him was just an itch to scratch, and as he'd gotten older, it was one he barely thought about anymore. He spread his hand out over his boy's smooth stomach, and his little finger dipped under the cotton of his boy's sleep pants. Tight, pubic curls teased the tip of his finger.

He pressed his lips to Derrick's ear. "We have to talk," he whispered low. He stroked his hand until he could fist his hand in the waist of the pants at Derrick's slim hip, he tugged, and Derrick got the idea. His boy rolled onto his back and helped him remove the pants. He had to be careful, or it would go too far. His gaze stroked down Derrick's chest, abdomen and lowered to a pretty cock in a nest of thick curls. When the fabric was tossed over the side of the bed, he barely acknowledged it too transfixed on the boy's gorgeous body. It wasn't perfect or ripped with muscle, but it was Derrick, and he loved the sight of it. He didn't think twice when he slipped his hand between Derrick's thighs and pushed his left leg to the side.

"Gage?"

Derrick's husky voice was filled with uncertainty, and he was ashamed when his cock jerked where it was pushed to Derrick's hip. It wasn't the first time he'd seen Derrick naked. He'd worked to get the boy comfortable with being exposed in front of people. Although, this time was different, they were alone and stretched out in bed. Cameras or not, it was just the two of them. Pure and Raul had gone to the room they were sharing in another part of the house.

"Fuck, you're beautiful." He cursed himself as soon as the words were out of his mouth. Derrick's warm breath fanned his bearded cheek, and all it would take was him turning his head for his mouth to be in the perfect spot to kiss his boy. He slowly drew his fingertips up Derrick's thigh, teased the start of his crease, taint and then cupped his boy's furry balls. Derrick gasped and arched his hips.

One kiss, that's all he wanted, so he turned his head, and his mouth brushed Derrick's trembling lips. He kissed the perfect bow of Derrick's top lip. Derrick's breath shuddered where it fanned his mouth. His mind emptied as he deepened the caress and rolled until he was cradled between his boy's thighs. It was everything he'd dreamed it would be, so easy with no awkwardness. He kept Derrick from feeling his hard-on, but his boy's dick was squeezed between their stomachs.

Their dual groans rang out too loudly in the room. He pressed his aching cock to the mattress needing just that bit of pressure. He felt the sweat start to bead on his skin. His arousal was stronger than at any time in his past. His boy spread wide beneath him, the painful gouge of Derrick's nails in his back caused his body to tense from his toes to shoulders.

"We can't do this," he whispered against Derrick's pretty lips, and even as he denied them their pleasure, his body took over. It was too much. Every dream he'd ever had was wrapped in his arms, writhing sweetly beneath him and he tore his mouth from Derrick's. He dragged his lips down the side of his boy's neck and sucked hard at his boy's pounding pulse. He was leaving a mark, and he didn't give a fuck—he wanted to cover Derrick in marks. He shoved his left hand between their bodies and pushed his fingertips to his boy's tight, clenching hole. "Tell me no, boy." Even as he ordered, he increased the pressure until the tip of his middle finger pushed into Derrick's body. "Do it, don't make me do something I'll regret."

He forced his gaze to Derrick's and the hurt there was obvious, but better to hurt him before they did something they couldn't take back. Derrick deserved someone to love him. God, how he wanted to be that man, to have the right to take him...claim him for his. Derrick's beautiful face was flushed, his pupils blown with pleasure.

"Why won't you love me?"

That question hurt, the boy didn't understand the depth of his obsession. He jerked his hand from between them and lifted slightly to shove his pants down to expose his cock. "Don't say I didn't warn you." He shifted until he notched their cocks together. He made sure the covers concealed their lower bodies.

"I promise I won't want more than this."

The lie was so clear that it pained him. He captured his boy's mouth, kissed him to the point of violence as he rutted against his beautiful boy. Derrick threw his head back breaking their kiss. He held onto a semblance of his control but all that shattered with one single word.

"Daddy!"

He rolled them until Derrick was on top. His cock pushed into the crease of Derrick's ass. He spat onto his left hand and started to jack his boy's cock. "Ride me, boy."

Derrick's nails dug into his chest, and he felt every time Derrick's hole brushed his cock. Derrick was arched above him, face to the ceiling and he'd never seen anything as beautiful. He sensed it in his soul that this sweet boy was made for him and he was so unworthy of Derrick. He grabbed Derrick's silky hair with his free hand and forced his boy down so he could reach his mouth. He's never craved kisses as much as he did with Derrick. As they rubbed their bodies together, he removed his grip from Derrick's cock and reached behind Derrick to fuck him raw with a single finger. It was too much and not enough, his boy whimpered and whispered Daddy repeatedly.

"Tonight, you're mine. I want to see you come." His hand slammed with such force against Derrick's ass that the slap resounded. "Tell Daddy how much you love being fucked by him. You asked for it." He released Derrick's hair, moved his boy up until his cock was free and his free hand fisted the cover at the small of Derrick's back. As his boy worked to get off, he took his own cock in hand, pressed the tip to Derrick's hole and jerked off. He wanted his boy to wear his scent.

Derrick hugged his neck, and he positioned his head close enough to Derrick's ear for the boy to hear every word. He didn't want to share any of that with anyone. If he could only savor this for one night, he was going to make sure Derrick knew it wasn't empty—that it meant more than just the pleasure of getting off. "Daddy has wanted you so long."

"Yes."

"You gonna cum for me, boy?"

Derrick only hummed an answer, and he noticed the moment his boy's body lost rhythm. He jacked his dick harder, almost painfully, imagined the grip of his boy's hole, precum barely enough to ease the friction. Derrick froze above him, and in the chaos, he'd pushed too hard, and the tip of his cock breached Derrick's tightness. Wetness spread between their bellies and the scent of sex became overwhelming—it was sweat and musk. He drew it deep into his lungs to memorize for the lonely times ahead. He gripped the base of his cock to keep from coming too soon. If tonight was all he got, he wanted everything. His boy was going to be sore from the lack of lube.

"Fuck, boy, so goddamn tight." The muscles reluctantly gave as he shallowly fucked his boy with the fat head of his dick and he barely jerked from Derrick's body before he spilled his seed all over Derrick's plump ass. He released the fabric from his hand, not caring if they were exposed. He massaged every drop of cum until the pleasure ebbed away. "I wanted every drop inside you. God, boy, you're going to break my fucking heart." He confessed with his mouth to Derrick's.

All thought of conversation about the job ended as his boy laid relaxed and sweaty on his chest. He didn't care about his sticky hand or the cum cooling on their skin. His arms embraced Derrick too tightly as he buried his face in the curve of his boy's shoulder. It was heaven and hell, everything he needed and knew he couldn't have. He whispered he was sorry not realizing his boy was still awake.

"It's okay. We'll be fine."

It was another bittersweet lie, and they both knew it, but neither of them acknowledged that. He had so many sins to pay for, but this was his greatest of all. Falling in love with Derrick was his darkest secret, and while he couldn't act upon it, that didn't mean he regretted it. He'd take whatever punishment he deserved when the operation was over. He would've sold what was left of his soul for this one night.

DERRICK HAD A LOT TO THINK ABOUT

*D*errick pretended not to watch Gage as the man packed up their things into the suitcase they shared. He'd already put Gage's suits back into the garment bag. Gage hadn't touched him again except to sleep or carry on the act, but the first night there still played repeatedly in his head. He regretted the promise he made. All he'd thought about for years was being loved on by Hayden Gage, and he'd had one night of belonging to the man. That morning, he'd awakened before Gage and looked down at the strong arm that had held him close, also the one under his head.

It had taken everything in him not to gasp at the neat rows of scars on the man's forearms. Some were pink enough to be only a few weeks old, and a couple still had scabs. He'd always found it odd that Gage wore long-sleeved shirts no matter the season. If he hadn't been so turned on, he probably would've noticed them the other night. He'd seen the scars of self-harm before. Quite a few of the Crews members had them. Unlike Gage's, they were pale, some hidden by tattoos.

He'd held still as not to wake Gage up, but he tenderly stroked each mark he could with the man's arms around him. At one point, he lifted his head slightly to brush his lips to them. He wondered if that's why Gage wouldn't let him close. As many cuts as he saw, he had a feeling those were only a few. Gage was the only man he'd ever wanted, and it broke him that his man suffered in silence—alone with a razor and his thoughts.

He didn't regret their night together or that he waited for Gage to be his first. That night made him realize that he would just have to be patient and let Gage know he wasn't going anywhere. Gage had to feel something for him, and when this operation was over, when they brought Cameron home, Gage was his. Yet first they had a job to do, and he wasn't looking forward to dealing with his dads. Crew didn't keep secrets, and what Gage and him did probably already made the rounds.

"Ready to go?"

He looked up to catch Gage's smile. "Yeah."

Pure and Raul walked in. They were still in their roles and came to take their bags. Pure had been unusually quiet. The man wasn't much of a talker, but something else was going on and he wondered if it was having to be there. Witnessing people walking around in practically nothing and being led around. Pure wasn't a prude, but something was bothering the man.

"We have information when we get out of here."

He watched as Raul and Gage exchanged looks, then they were on the move. Gage in front, him behind followed by the other two men. He hadn't been left alone in days, and he was looking forward to a bit of privacy back at the hotel. Maybe a shower where he knew he wasn't being watched. They descended the steps and Forester was waiting at the bottom.

"Hayden, Derrick, could I have a moment in my office?"

The man appeared friendly enough, and Gage and Forester seemed to bond over their conversations. Last night had been slightly embarrassing, his ass and back were still tender from the lash of the flogger Gage had used on him. They'd discussed the scene, and Gage had promised if he said no, that they wouldn't do it. Gage had taken such care when securing him to the cross. Made sure that he was covered so that no one could see his dick. With his forehead leaned on the cross he could ignore everyone but Gage.

He was hoping one day that they could have another night with the flogger in a more private setting.

"Of course."

Gage motioned him forward and placed his hand on Derrick's lower back. He let Gage lead him to the office, following Forester. Once they were inside, Forester closed the doors, and it was just the two of them.

"In the years I've been doing this, I've never been informed of someone watching my home. I did some checking on Trenton Security when I was informed, and it's a business with some rather...colorful headlines attached to it and the facial recognition I did on the man positioned a mile away comes back to an Alex Quintin. Former Navy man. Runs Quintin Investments with his former girlfriend. They have a daughter who was reported missing not long ago."

"You're pretty good with running a search," Gage said. His tone was free of emotion. Gage hadn't even tensed.

"If you had approached me in the beginning, I would've allowed you full access. If you went through all the trouble of creating a false identity to get into my home, it must be important."

"As you already know, Alex Quintin's daughter disappeared. We've been tracking down information on auctions and private acquisitions. Your event came up as a point of interest. We built the fake identity to join your event on the off-chance that you purchased Cameron."

"We're a very private group of individuals, and while our get-togethers are secret, there is nothing in the least illegal about consenting adults agreeing to have some fun. Yes, the young men and women are paid to be here, but they're paid quite well. As you learned, I show them the greatest respect."

"I know, but you have to understand we had to try. Every other lead was a bust."

"You didn't get this from me," Forester said as he turned to pick up a thumb drive from the desk.

When the man turned around, the expression was all wrong.

"As I told you the other night, we occasionally check to make sure that our guests aren't being abusive. I was called down to our security office in the middle of the night and shown a tape of an incident that happened. When I spoke with one of the participates, I decided to use the information that I learned about you."

"What's on it?" Gage took the drive.

"I typically don't worry about what happens outside my home, but one of my guests brought abhorrent behavior here. Francois and another of the guests used Kray in a disgusting manner. It was quite clear they didn't have his consent to do so. Security followed me to the room. I informed both that they were to leave and Kray would remain with me. I threatened to call the cops if he wasn't, but unfortunately, as far as I know, Kray is an adult and filming people is also against the law, he chose to leave with Francois. I will pay quite well for you to remove him from the situation he's in. I've been told by a few people that you've done several jobs in the past that were less than legal."

The horror and sadness on Forester's face was clear, and he was sure the guilt was eating the man up. They'd already agreed to follow Francois and rescue the young man.

"We'd already planned on it. Do you know anything about him? Anything would help."

"Francois Arsenault has a company in New York City, but has

a home outside the city. He has dual citizenship and regularly travels outside the country. A file I have of his personal stats, addresses, contact information are all on the drive."

"When did they leave?"

"They were escorted off the property at four a.m. and were followed to the airport."

"What isn't on the drive?"

"He's a very powerful man. Friends in every level of government and business, and I have a feeling that's why he gets away with what he does. It has been mentioned several times in the past he has collected an impressive harem and last night proves the rumor I heard true that he likes to share. If you're looking for someone who may have purchased someone, again merely speculation, he's done it in the past.

"Hayden, I will say be careful with this one. Don't just go in demanding, I can tell you, he's the type of man to make problems disappear. Kray doesn't deserve to have his life cut short before he's actually had a chance to live one."

The tension in the room amped up to the point that it was oppressive. his brain was only thinking of what Kray suffered, probably was suffering. That French fucker could've already gotten rid of Kray. Gage asked a few more questions, and Forester willingly answered every one. They didn't waste time returning to Pure and Raul, and then they were in the limo and on the way back to the hotel in no time. Gage already had his phone out talking to Linus, and Pure and Raul were coordinating with the rest of team on the new direction of the mission.

Could it be that simple? Luck played a big role in solving crimes all the time, and if they could save Kray and Cameron, he didn't care how it happened. If the bastard was as dangerous as Forester made out, then there could be more people suffering. They made plans and had it all in motion before the car pulled up in front of their hotel.

The look on Linus' face didn't bode well for when they were alone, but he didn't have time to think about that. They had a meeting to get to, and he'd deal with the fall out later. He was an adult, and he had no issues with what happened. When the time came, he'd tell them exactly that.

WHEN GAGE FUCKED UP, HE WENT ALL OUT

"*I* didn't fucking send my son to you so you could fuck him." Linus' voice was dangerously calm.

He was waiting for the other man to throw a punch, but it hadn't happened yet. He hadn't meant for their act to shift into more. Yet he wouldn't regret it happened. He still remembered the heat and tightness of Derrick's hole around the head of his dick. When he fucked up, he made it one for the books. Derrick was avoiding him anyway. Maybe the boy came to his senses and figured out that he wasn't worth the effort. He mentally growled at his own thoughts. Wasn't that what he wanted? When the operation inside Forester's house ended, so did the act. It had made him admit things to himself that he'd ignored over the years—he'd fallen in love, and it wouldn't work out between him and his boy. He had too many secrets to make it fair to Derrick.

"I didn't fuck him. We had to talk while being watched. I wouldn't have gotten the information I needed if we made Forester suspicious." He didn't need to explain anything to Linus, and while their moment hadn't been private, he wouldn't lay out the details, especially not to his fucking boss.

"Apparently, your act wasn't good enough because he made y'all within hours."

"That might be true, but he gave us the information we needed. We've solved shit by luck before."

"Gage, we have to be realistic, Alex..."

"Alex is fine. Hope is not a bad thing. I'm going to find Cameron no matter what it takes. I can do this on my own."

"Shut the fuck up. You're not doing anything alone. And while we have some privacy, don't fuck with my son. If you ain't keeping him leave him the fuck alone. Are we understood?"

He clenched his back teeth and prepared himself to lie. Hadn't he already promised himself that he would leave Derrick alone? It was torture to be in the same room with him. For nearly a week, he'd had the freedom to touch his boy in any way he wanted. He'd memorized every inch of Derrick. Every freckle or mole, pale scars were committed to memory. He knew what the stripes of pink welts from a flogger looked like in contrast to Derrick's lightly tanned back and ass.

"Gage, you're one of my best friends, but you've...you've pulled away the last few years. You got your secrets, we all do, but this being a parent shit sucks a lot of the time, and I don't want my son hurt. He's already had enough pain growing up."

"Ain't shit going on, man. Derrick has a talent for undercover work. He was made to work law enforcement."

The pride that took over Linus' expression couldn't be mistaken for anything else. "I wanted to offer him a job with us, but he wants to prove something to Powers. That he isn't his bastard father. I support it even if I don't like it. I will warn you, sleep light around Hunter. He wants blood."

He shook his head and knew Hunter was more protective of Derrick, Linus would take him out because it upset his husband. He wasn't stupid enough to think that this was the end of the discussion. Once the operation was over, he'd probably pay for supposedly taking advantage of Derrick.

"What's the plan?"

"We're setting up a base of operation near Arsenault's residence. Margo, Little and Livingston are already on their way. We need to have a meeting with Alex, and he's waiting for us in the living room. Gage, we have to be honest with him about this. All our leads have dried up, and unless they left from a private airstrip, then she's still stateside."

"I know, man. I do. Let me take the lead."

"You're on point for this one. Once we're together, though, there's some information on the boy."

He nodded and took a deep breath as they both exited his room. Derrick was taking up one side of the couch, crossed leg as Derrick scrolled through something on the tablet he was holding. Alex looked thinner, and his handsome face was marred with a permanent frown. He was about to destroy his best friend's hopes. Raul was leaned back on a dining table a few feet behind where Pure was seated on the floor cleaning his rifle. Pure hadn't spoken to him since they'd left the estate. They'd have to have a private conversation soon. If they couldn't work as a team, it would put all of them in danger.

"Alex," he called his friend's name and took a seat on the coffee table in front of where Alex sat. "We have to talk."

"My baby isn't dead."

"I'm not saying she is, but leads have dried up. She could've been smuggled out of the states. There's ways to do so. Alex, we have to prepare for the worst."

"How the fuck am I going to tell Margo? I promised to bring her home, and I fucking failed."

Alex clenched his fists, and Gage laid his hands over them. The tears that were streaming down Alex's face killed him. He'd promised Alex the same thing—that he'd bring Cameron home. They were suffocating under the weight of their guilt. He remembered the moment she was born, the weight of her the first time they'd allowed him to hold his goddaughter. The joyous sound of her sweet laughter. She'd never known fear believing they'd always protect her and they'd failed her. If she wasn't dead, he was terrified of the girl they'd get back. How broken would their Cameron be?

"I have to know, Gage, either way. At least give us closure, I don't want my baby laying out there alone."

He wrapped his left hand around the back of Alex's neck and pulled the man to him. Strong arms wrapped around him and he bit back his own tears as his friend sobbed, clutching at the back of his shirt. He turned his head to kiss the side of Alex's neck and waited while Alex broke and mourned.

"Alex." Linus' voice came from too close.

He turned his head to find Linus crouched down beside them, and Alex shifted to look at Linus, too.

"We'll find your baby, and dead or alive, those fuckers will suffer. You've worked with us, became a member of our Crew and with that, we take care of our own. They fucked with one of us. We can't make the decision for you, you tell us now, do you want their heads?"

"Yes."

Linus nodded and straightened. "We leave in a few hours, Alex, why don't you go get some rest."

"I want to hear the rest. What about the boy?" Alex asked.

He almost protested but figured his friend needed a distraction. He spun to take a seat on the couch between Alex and Derrick, and he didn't miss the pressure of a knee and toes against the side of his thigh. He glanced at Derrick to find the boy giving him a small, reassuring smile and he appreciated the silent support.

"The boy was abandoned at the hospital. All reports say he was born prematurely addicted to heroin and wasn't expected to survive. Kray Doe. He was reported as a runaway two years ago at the age of fourteen. He didn't return to the group home after skipping school."

"So, he's sixteen?" he asked.

"Yep, in the end, he was just another runaway and cops didn't think twice about writing him off. He was taken off the streets in Houston. There's nothing. Apparently, his birth mother didn't give her real name. As soon as she was left alone, she snuck out. He was court ordered to become a ward of the state."

"No one took him?" Alex's shock deepened his voice.

"Man, they expected him to die within hours of birth, and he had health issues. He wasn't perfect."

"Doesn't mean no one could take him. He was just a baby." Alex's shock had turned to anger, and Gage loved that for at least a moment his best friend had his fire back.

"Do we know if there are others?" Derrick asked.

He watched Derrick lean forward to place his tablet on the table and then shift until his back was to the arm of the couch. His boy looked tired, and he wanted to tell Derrick to go lie down, but it wasn't his place to care for Derrick.

"What we could find is Arsenault has some pretty shady friends, and more than a few have been charged but never prosecuted for using underaged prostitutes. So we're sure they're pedophiles. I want to take them all down." Linus growled and clenched his fists.

"We can't have a lot of bodies on this one, Linus. One or two, we can spin that shit that we were sent in to extract a client's daughter and things went sideways." He knew they didn't give a shit about the body count. It wouldn't be the first time they buried a body in the desert. They weren't above vigilante justice when the operation called for extreme prejudice.

"Hunter is gathering every bit of information that they find. Evidence in the way of encrypted communications and suspicious activity in offshore accounts. He's following the money trail. It will be turned over to a contact Pelter has in the FBI for them to build a case, but Arsenault, he dies and anyone with him."

Everyone in the room agreed, and they finalized a few plans. But as they were all about to go their own direction, Alex stood and squared his shoulders. "I want Kray," he announced strongly, his voice was filled with conviction Gage rarely heard from him.

"What?" He shifted to look at his best friend.

"Peaches can arrange everything, right? I want the papers in place for me to take custody. I'll put her in contact with my lawyer. Money isn't an problem. That boy is going to have a family no matter what I have to do."

"Alex, don't be rash, this isn't the time to..."

"Linus, I've seen the pictures. When he gets rescued, they're going to lock him up or throw him back into some group home. They won't give a fuck about him, and I won't let that fucking happen."

"I'll get you in contact with Peaches. She doesn't do family law, but I think she might be able to work something out. Don't get your hopes up."

"That's all I've heard for weeks, and I'm tired of it. Make it happen. I don't care what you have to do."

He started to call Alex's name, but the man left the room without another word. He watched the man's broad back as he disappeared. When he glanced at Linus, he found the man staring straight at him.

"Is your man there going to keep his shit together?" Linus asked.

"He'll be fine. I suggest we all get some rest, but first I'd like to talk to Pure in private."

The room cleared out as he met Pure's glare from the big man's seat on the floor. Pure gently laid his rifle on the towel spread out that he was working on and he took the three steps that separated them. He lowered to the carpet. The rage in the other man's eyes was so foreign because Pure was always the most controlled of them all. To do the job Pure did, the man needed nerves of steel.

"We have to work this shit out. Whatever it is we have to talk."

"Nothing to talk about."

"Bullshit, Pure. This operation fucked with you and I need to know why. It's just between the two of us."

"Did you like hurting him?" Pure's asked coldly.

"I didn't hurt Derrick."

"You spanked him. Exposed him so other people could look at him. That's not respectful."

"How long have you worked with us, Pure?"

"What's that gotta do with anything?"

"Have any of the partners of the Crew ever acted as if something they do together is shameful?"

Pure glanced away. "No."

"What partners do together, as long as it's safe, sane and consensual is okay. I know there's more going on with you than you just wanting to wait for the right man to come along. What Derrick and I did was part of the operation. Your wishes were respected because it was something you weren't comfortable with and we'd never take that choice away from you."

"Did he like what you did?"

"Between you and me?" Pure just nodded. "I hope so because I don't regret it. We all have our secrets. Shit, we won't share, and mine are a bit darker than most. If I was a different man, I'd try to make that boy mine, but that's not possible. There's something broken inside me...a part of myself that I don't know if I'll ever be able to control. If you ever want to talk about what you're hiding, you say the word. No one else would need to know."

"I'm sorry, I know y'all have this whole sexual freedom thing going and sometimes I'm jealous of it. I just want a man who'll love me and not leave when I've served my purpose."

"And you wait for that, that's what you deserve. Are we good though?"

"I was an asshole, we're good."

"I think being on this team requires you to be an asshole. Get some rest. You look like you need it."

"Yeah, I don't sleep real good in strange places, and Raul snores."

He laughed loudly as Pure's impish grinned returned, and the tension eased from him. He wasn't sure if they were completely back on the same page, but it was good enough for now. He pushed up from the floor and returned to his room. He needed a nap, but he doubted if he'd sleep. Too much was clouding his head—Derrick, where Cameron was and the new operation to get Kray. He was going to take a nice long vacation when all this shit was over. He was getting too old for this shit.

DERRICK HATED STAKEOUT DUTY

*L*ittle was on the other side of the enclosed space with his phone pressed to his ear and whispering dirty talk to Poe. Livingston was smirking at his tablet on the other side. He didn't want to know what Liv was watching because he was sure it had something to do with Fielding with no clothes on. He was put in charge of watching the monitors while the other two men said goodnight to their men. Okay, he'd admit he was a little jealous. As soon as they'd landed, they'd been mission ready. And since they'd arrived at the suite the day before after leaving Forester's, he hadn't found a minute to talk to Gage.

Occasionally he found Gage watching him, but as soon as their eyes met, the other man looked away. He didn't let it bother him too much. His plan was when they returned to Powers that they'd have a private talk where they weren't worried about someone interrupting. He smiled as he raised his hand and tugged at the tiny lock on his collar. Gage hadn't removed it yet, and even if he wanted to, Gage still had the key hanging around his neck. He was dreading the day Gage asked for it back.

He loved where it was, and he could pretend that everything would work out when everything there ended. Two growly moans made him push his chair back against the far wall and point at the two fuckers he was trapped with.

"One of you even looks like you're gonna grab your dick, I'm out."

"Don't be jealous we get to have our sexy men say goodnight and your old man is out there in his gear with his big ol' gun."

"Fuck you, Little," he grumbled as he flipped off the crazy man.

They weren't wrong. Being away and Gage pulling out of the field, he'd never had the opportunity to see Gage in his tactical gear. Gage had entered the main room where they were running the operation. Gage had been dressed in all black, Bail Enforcement Agent across the back of the bulletproof vest. The pants had hugged the muscular curves of Gage's perfect ass. His Glock was in a thigh holster and he wanted to tackle the man and drag him in the nearest room with a lock. Gage looked sexy as fuck in his suits, but in his gear, it was instant hard-on.

His Daddy was definitely wearing that the next spanking he earned, and he thought of all the ways he could have Daddy punish him. He wasn't a stranger to a man in uniform, and none of them affected him the way Gage had just walking into the room.

He'd only done a double-take over Alex once because the man looked so odd out of his thousand-dollar suits and his expensive casual wear. Alex looked elegant whatever he wore while Gage appeared dangerous. He could develop a fetish for Gage all decked out for a takedown.

They'd run a week of recon on Arsenault's home and businesses. The bastard was a creature of habit. Left for work at the same time every day. Went to a private club for drinks and a lap dance before returning home. He'd had several guests over the week. Not once had they seen Kray or evidence of any other captives in the house. They were trying to get someone in to place cameras and bugs, but the fucker had more security measures than they'd thought for a residential home. Arsenault had things to hide—he had no doubt about that. Hunter had tried to tap into the signal, but the only cameras he could get access to were the ones around the perimeter of the house and nothing on the inside.

Headlights appeared as the doors of the garage opened and the car that Arsenault used drove up to the front of the house. He tapped his earpiece.

"We have movement."

"Team One be ready to move." Linus' voice was low in his ear.

Raul had the best experience to enter the house without notice, and they'd timed the patrols. Arsenault never left the house without at least two bodyguards. They'd run facial recognition on all of them, and each one had some tie to organized crime or spent a good portion of their lives in prison. These were men who wouldn't think twice about shooting first.

"Sniper, you have eyes?" he asked.

"Affirmative, on your command."

Pure was positioned at the back of the house where Raul would make entry. "I want eyes on." They identified themselves as the monitors lit up with infrared images, and once Raul made entry, they'd switch his camera. Arsenault's security team would return to a guest house out back where they ran their operation, and he kept his eyes on the camera. They'd have a twenty-minute window for Raul to get in, place the cameras with mics, and then get back out before the next round.

Linus ordered radio silence as Arsenault and his bodyguards left, then they sat there impatiently waiting for the next patrol. He counted bodies, and the last guard disappeared inside the small cottage.

"Team One move."

It was nerve-wracking to wait and just watch Raul's progress. Linus, Gage, and Little would cover Raul, Pure would oversee taking anyone out, and the others would extract Raul if needed.

Raul avoided every camera and approached a side door, then the man turned the handle and made entry. The lights were out, and Raul kept low as he moved through the rooms.

"Fuck, we got a man inside...Raul hug the wall." He barely caught movement at the backdoor. They had an extra man that hadn't been accounted for this week.

"Did the fucker hire extra security?" Livingston was right beside him staring at the cameras.

"It appears so, but I don't know how the hell we missed him." He was pissed at himself for missing that. He held his breath as the big guy in the cheap suit made a round of the house from the new camera that he'd brought online. Raul skirted the edges of the rooms and hallways staying behind the guy patrolling the house.

"None of us caught it, don't beat yourself up over it."

Raul's camera lowered as the man crouched down and tried the handle of a door he was leaning against. "We have a locked door. Appears to lead down to a basement. Should I chance it?"

He remained silent as he waited for Linus or Gage to answer. From the outside of the house there appeared to be no exit from the basement. One way in or out was dangerous especially when they were outnumbered. The Trenton Team were some of the best, but Raul would be trapped and depending on what or who was in the basement, they couldn't chance civilian casualties.

"Negative. I'm not going to chance it yet," Linus responded.

He checked his watch. "You have five minutes." Raul needed to make his way out now, or his chances of detection increased.

The man straightened and moved around, placing the last of the equipment. The last one was in Arsenault's upstairs bedroom, and with barely a minute to spare, Raul exited through his entry point. The darkness shielded him.

"We're on the move," Gage said.

He killed the dim light in the van waiting for the team to return and the back door creaked open. Too many bodies crowded inside. Pure was the only one that held position. They'd placed a signal booster, and while the house was in the middle of nowhere, their motel was close enough to read the signals. "Hunter, do you have eyes?"

"Yes, I do. You did good gentlemen. Although you could've tried not to make it so close. I'd like my husband home in one piece."

"What about me, Dad?"

"You too, Derrick."

"Derrick, Little and Livingston, I'll need y'all to stay here until we're sure everything is working at base. I want the three of you back at the motel before dawn. A few more days and we're going in, I need everyone rested and fucking ready," Linus ordered.

Calloused fingertips stroked along the chain where it rested on the back of his neck, and he bit back a groan as it was pulled slightly. The lock dug into his skin. Little started laughing then covered it with a cough. *Asshole.* He needed new friends. Too quickly the pressure ceased, and the cramped interior cleared out.

"When you two actually get around to fucking, you're going to kill each other." Little barely got the words out through his laughter.

"Little, I'll kill you and hide your body with Arsenault's." Gage's growled.

"Fuck," he hissed and quickly cut communications as Little made sounds like a dying hyena beside him. "You're such an asshole, Little."

"Dude, you should be thanking me, that fuck of yours could earn you a spanking. Daddies don't like when they're boys have dirty mouths."

He removed his earpiece and threw it at Little. Linus and Hunter weren't making a big deal about what happened at Forester's, and he'd like to keep it that way. They'd keep everything professional until the operation ended and then he knew there were no guarantees. He slumped down in the uncomfortable chair and kept his gaze glued to the monitors.

HIS STOMACH KNOTTED with nerves a few hours later when Arsenault returned and went straight for the locked basement door.

Every horrific act that could be occurring in that room played through his head and by the time Arsenault reappeared he was ready to puke.

"We'll get him out, and we'll find Cameron, we don't give up once we start," Livingston whispered only loud enough to be heard over Little's soft snores.

"I know, but the longer we take to make sure everything is safe for us to move in, the more that boy is probably being abused."

"Arsenault dies, and Kray gets to watch as we slowly destroy the fucker. It's the only closure we can give him, but the monsters will be dead. It's up to him to move on."

"I hope so. Any news on Cameron?"

"The Jane Doe that turned up on Miami Beach wasn't her. I guess that's good news for us and bad news for someone else. Get a few minutes of sleep. I'll take over watching the monitors. My boy will be calling in a few minutes."

He just nodded and slipped off the chair to let Livingston take his place, and then he curled up in a nest of blankets. He wouldn't sleep, but he'd try to close his eyes for a few. When this nightmare was over, he'd catch up on his sleep then.

HIS BOY LOOKED EXHAUSTED

*G*age tried to rub the sleep from his eyes with one hand and set his half-eaten breakfast on the floor with the other. He winced as the tape pulled at his arm hair. The bandage was new and the cut deeper than it was supposed to be —he'd felt shame the moment the razor sliced his skin. He tried to sleep, but nightmares had filled his head. The same one that he always had. His mother's glassy eyes and a bathtub filled with blood, the Major's voice telling him that they needed to know their place.

The stress of the operation and his inability to let Derrick go ate at him until he'd needed a release. Pain cleared his head, but unlike all the times before, he didn't feel that rush of euphoria at the sting. Agony was safe. Happiness was dangerous and tainted the rage that existed just below the surface. He wanted to be different so that he knew he wasn't capable of hurting Derrick.

What happened if he lost his temper and he lost his sense of reality? A long time had passed since he'd lost it. Yet, he felt it was only a matter of time.

Everyone around him seemed as if they were at the point of collapse. Nerves were frayed. Alex and Margo were curled up on the bed, cuddled together for comfort. They'd went their separate ways a few years ago when she'd met someone on a blind date. He'd always found their open relationship odd. Alex loved her, but he'd been away so much during their relationship that it was probably for the best. When Alex had explained everything, Margo had instantly agreed that Kray would have a place with them.

Hunter and Linus were in an opposite corner having a video call with Wren and Pride. Little and Livingston were off doing whatever they do, and Pure and Raul were manning the van. They'd all been going twenty-four hours a day since all this started with maybe what added up to naps. He didn't know what possessed him, but when he caught Derrick's gaze, he motioned his boy over. His boy stumbled a bit getting to his feet.

"Come on, since you won't go to your room, sit here."

Derrick plopped down between his legs, and his boy laid his head on his knee. He gently combed his fingers through Derrick's hair, and as his boy sighed, he smiled. He shifted until Derrick's head rested on his inner thigh and Derrick wrapped himself around his leg. Without analyzing it, he rested his head on the back of the uncomfortable chair and closed his eyes.

The more he told himself that he wasn't going to lead Derrick on, the more he couldn't resist. He couldn't blame it on the Crews being close. They'd curled up together more times than he could count when they were off on jobs. It wasn't something they thought twice about, but with Derrick, the pull was too strong. Every time he had a free moment his thoughts went back to their nights together. It was almost of if he were addicted to sleeping with his boy in his arms.

No matter that it would be safer for Derrick to stay far away from him, he was selfish for whatever time he could steal. When they were back to their real lives, their paths wouldn't cross as much. He felt the impression of the key and chain around his neck, and he knew people were speculating about why he hadn't asked for the collar back. The chain had always belonged to Derrick. He was the person he'd had in mind when he'd purchased it. Never had he dreamed Derrick would wear it or that he would catch his boy playing with the lock.

The night they'd placed the cameras, he scented his boy, and he'd been close enough to inhale it deep into his lungs. When he'd curled his fingers around the chain and pulled, he'd heard the smallest gasp that Derrick had bit back before he thought anyone heard. Little's laughter proved that he hadn't hidden what he'd done. His newest favorite fantasy was his boy bent over his desk. Controlling his boy with the chain as he pounded his lush ass.

Even as exhausted as he was, his cock responded to the thought. To save himself embarrassment, he thought about the mission at hand. In a few short hours, they'd start taking out the guards one by one before they stormed the house. They couldn't leave Kray inside any longer. Every night they steeled themselves to wait for Arsenault to return to the basement. Luckily for them, he hadn't returned after the night they planted the equipment. That didn't mean they hadn't had to endure the violence that happened in the fucker's bedroom. Men and women, most of them barely looked legal, and they'd taken the money Arsenault handed over quick enough. The background checks they'd run on Arsenault's bed partners showed they were of age and were known for taking on clients with rougher tastes. That didn't make it any easier to take.

Pure was barely holding on to his sanity. The big man was quiet to begin with, but since they began the surveillance, Pure seemed to have lost some of his light. He tried to talk Linus into sending Pure back to Powers, but the big man claimed he was fine. It was a lie, and they all knew it.

He felt his lids getting heavier and sleep approached whether he wanted it to or not. As he felt himself drift to sleep a smile curved his mouth with the feel of Derrick's arms circling his waist and the weight of his boy's head on his lower stomach.

Sleeping with Derrick was the best he'd ever had, and he'd enjoy it one more night no matter how uncomfortable the position.

IT WAS FUCKING CHAOS, each guard they knocked unconscious and secured with zip ties amped up their impatience. So far it appeared as if they hadn't alerted the others and they only had another five men to take out. Unfortunately, it appeared as if they'd have to make entry. Derrick and Pure's voices alerted them to every movement and position of the enemy. None of them spoke, and masks concealed their faces. They covered Bail Enforcement with black tape that could be removed when needed. Peaches had arrived right before they left the hotel and was waiting for their word to inform the authorities.

That was as close to legal as the operation was getting. Some of the men they'd taken down had bounties which meant they had a semblance of an excuse to be there. They swept the rest of the yard then moved as a unit toward the back door. Linus held up his arm and counted down from three, then they busted inside, and Alex was at his six. They separated into teams, bellows and curses filled the house as the rest of Arsenault's men were neutralized.

They fought long and hard against Alex taking part in the breach, but in the end, they decided it was his right. Privately, Linus had told him Alex was his responsibility. They made their way upstairs to clear the top floor. Derrick's voice in his ear said Arsenault had headed downstairs minutes before they entered. They were told to converge at the basement door. He had volunteered to take point, and he held his breath as he turned the knob. As he pulled it open the hinges barely made a sound, but the cries from downstairs were loud enough.

It was at least two people crying, and Arsenault was taunting them.

"Who wants to play with Sir first?" The bastard's voice was slurred.

"Me, leave her alone, I'll do whatever you want." A squeaky male voice stuttered out each word.

"Maybe I should break her in some more. You two can perform for me finally. Both my pets fucking for me."

"No, no, I'll do whatever you want, she's sick, please."

The stairs creaked under his boots as he slowly made it down. The boy he assumed was Kray was protecting at least one other person down there. He crouched low enough to check the situation. The boy had a girl hidden behind his thin frame. Kray wasn't in any shape to defend anyone but was offering himself up to protect his cellmate. He was in motion as soon as the fucker started undoing his belt.

"I'd rethink that if I were you." He pressed the barrel of his semi-automatic rifle to the base of the fucker's skull. "On your knees, now, cross your ankles."

"You won't make it out of this house alive." The man's arrogance clear.

Alex covered Arsenault as he secured his hands with a tie behind his back. "Every one of your men is currently incapacitated. All clear," he yelled up the steps. "Find me blankets. We have two friendlies."

As he straightened and moved into the cell, the scent of unwashed flesh and the mustiness of the basement made him snarl his nose. Kray was instantly wrapped around the girl, using his almost skeletal frame to lie completely on top of her. He didn't attempt to touch them just knelt slowly beside them. Both of them were naked, and their bodies were covered in blood and dirt, and who the hell knew what else.

"Kray, we're here to get you out. You've been missing for two years. We're going to get you and your friend blankets, then we're going to lead you out. You're free."

"Free?"

The hope in those hazel eyes filled with tears killed him because he still possessed hope but suspicious enough not to believe him.

"Kray, where are you and your friend hurt?"

"Everywhere."

"What's your friend's name?"

"Cameron, she hasn't been here long."

All hell broke loose as Alex was on the ground ripping his mask off. "Baby, Cameron?" Because Kray wouldn't release Cameron, they were both caught up in Alex's arms. Cameron was suddenly crying and screaming Dad. Kray looked confused and terrified to be trapped.

"Blankets. Is the fucker coming with us? We scoped out a place for his body."

"You're all dead. Lay one fucking finger on me..." Arsenault didn't have a chance to finish as he turned to find Linus who laid the fucker out with one punch.

They'd all agreed that Arsenault wouldn't make it through the night and they'd only inform the authorities after the fucker was dead and buried. It was one death that they wouldn't mind having on them. He'd be just another rich bastard that had escaped to a non-extradition country to avoid prosecution.

"I informed the rest of the team that we had Kray and Cameron."

"Put him in the trunk." He stayed crouched down as Alex and Cameron kept crying while he occasionally checked her over. He slipped Kray out of the embrace and gently wrapped him in a blanket. Every bone was displayed under bruised skin, and he didn't know how the kid was still alive.

Arsenault was carried from the basement, and he'd be placed in the trunk of his own car. Him and Linus would be the only ones to do away with the bastard. They'd already discussed it. Livingston had already dug a shallow grave.

"Am I really free?"

"Yes. You'll be taken to a hospital to be treated."

"Where will I go, I got nowhere."

"We'll worry about that later. First let's get you patched up, then a hot bath and meal."

It took two of them to get Alex and Cameron to their feet—they clung so tightly to each other making it up the narrow staircase was awkward. His relief at finding Cameron was only eclipsed by the horror of what she'd suffered in that basement. There were some things that even time couldn't heal. Kray and Cameron had a long road ahead of them. Pure and Raul would stay with the guards they'd taken out until the cops arrived.

He stood back to watch the headlights of the van disappear. "You ready for this?" he asked Linus.

"He won't stop unless someone takes him out. My conscience is clear."

It was all he needed to hear, and they got in the car. They drove in the opposite direction an hour away to the spot where Arsenault would die. He felt no guilt or shame over what he was about to do. Vengeance was justified when they knew the system was rigged toward the rich and powerful. The fucker had too many friends in high places. The story would be Arsenault escaped in the operation to take down several fugitives, and it was the story they were sticking to.

DERRICK HADN'T BEEN PREPARED

They were all packed into the emergency waiting room as they assessed Kray and Cameron. Security had already threatened to kick Alex out if he didn't keep his temper under control. Peaches was herding the cops and giving them the paperwork on every fugitive they'd snagged that night. Everyone that entered the house had told the same story that Arsenault had run with a few of his security people. A rental vehicle was parked about a five-mile hike from where they'd bury Arsenault.

The longer that Gage and Linus were away from the group, the more anxious he became. He paced to keep his mind off what was going on, but it didn't help. He wanted his man back so that he could look at him and make sure he was okay. The two men had taken the task of doing away with the sadistic bastard to save the conscience of everyone else. He didn't think anyone else would shed a tear about putting a bullet between the fucker's eyes. He'd almost volunteered to do it himself.

When they'd brought Kray out of the house, he'd looked even skinnier than he had when he'd seen him at Forester's. The doctor taking care of Kray had come out and asked who was there for him. They'd all stepped forward, and the doctor had taken a step back. The Trenton team did make a scary picture in their all black gear. At least they'd thought to leave their weapons in the van.

"No, I'm asking who his parents are, I can only speak to a guardian."

"I'm his advocate and attorney." Peaches stepped forward with a piece of paper. "Mr. Alex Quintin is in the process of petitioning for temporary custody until he can apply to adopt."

He didn't know how the hell she pulled the shit that she did. Peaches had a shadier history than all the Crews combined. He didn't ask too many questions because he didn't want to know. The doctor led Peaches and Alex to a quiet corner. Margo had been allowed back to stay with Cameron. Alex had reluctantly agreed to wait to learn more about Kray.

"Kray is suffering from severe malnutrition and dehydration. He's had significant sexual trauma. The x-rays show that he's had several broken bones that weren't healed properly. He wouldn't have lasted another month in the condition he was. We're doing an HIV test and also checking for other STDs. We need to do a rape kit but…"

He didn't know why he stepped forward, but he didn't want the kid alone, and maybe a familiar face would help.

"I'm a deputy, I've assisted with sexual assault exams before." He stepped forward a little further. "If Kray would be okay with it, we can ask him." He was closer to Kray's age and wasn't built on a massive scale, and he wasn't really a stranger.

"We need him to stay calm. We'll be as quick as possible, but we need the evidence if his attacker is ever found."

"Couldn't hurt to ask."

Peaches caught his hand as he passed and he inhaled slowly through his nose and out through his mouth to calm his nerves. The curtain that concealed Kray parted only far enough for them to enter.

"Hello, Kray."

The kid was curled into a fetal position on the narrow gurney, and he didn't get close enough to touch. He wanted to take Kray in his arms and hold him close because he had a feeling no one had held him before. He sure hadn't received a sliver of kindness in nearly two years.

"I know you."

"Yeah, we didn't get the chance to introduce ourselves. I'm Deputy Derrick Thorpe."

"You were with the older guy with kind eyes. He was very nice to you."

"Yeah, he was. The doctor said that you're anxious about them checking you and I've assisted with a few exams. And I'm not big and scary like the rest of them. I can just hold your hand and talk to you."

"Will they stop if I say so?"

"If they don't, I have some very scary men with guns, one of them is my dad." He relaxed his tensed shoulder when that earned him the tiniest smile. "So, what do you say?"

"Okay."

He approached the bed and slid one of the chairs closer to take a seat. He held out his hand and two thin, trembling hands took his. "They'll put your legs up, and there will be a sheet, you won't see a thing they do."

"Am I really free?"

"Yes, and I have it on a very good authority that you have a very nice place to go."

"I don't want to go back to the home. They didn't like me there."

"We'll talk about that all later."

Tears filled Kray's beautiful eyes, and when the kid tensed, he held tighter to his hand. "Talk to me."

"Is Cameron okay? I tried to protect her. I promise I did."

"Hey, calm down, she's in another room, and she's being taken care of by her mom."

"She told me about her mom and dad, they sounded amazing."

He talked and listened, he soothed and made the doctor stop whenever it got to be too much. Minutes felt like hours, and when the exam ended and exhaustion made Kray pass out, he stayed there holding the kid's hand. He stroked the limp, ginger curls back from the beautiful little face. He looked so much younger in his sleep. He lifted his head when he heard the curtain move and found Margo standing there.

"Is it okay to come in?" she asked.

"Yeah, I think he's out for the count. How's Cameron?"

"They sedated her. She had a panic attack and couldn't catch her breath. Alex is sitting with her. We rented two of the biggest suites we could find for everyone. It'll be a while before they can travel. Some of you will have to bunk up together, but I don't think some of you will protest."

"What are the cops saying?"

"That Trenton Security is either very good or very, very crazy. They've set up checkpoints from here to the airport and are distributing his information as a person of interest."

"Have Linus and Gage shown up yet?"

"The cops are taking their statements now. Peaches is going to act as advocates for Kray and Cameron. She's pretty scary."

"That's putting it lightly. I wasn't prepared for any of this. I've heard all the stories of the Trenton team riding to the rescue, but how can they do this every day?"

"It's takes exceptional men to do what they do. I've heard stories from Gage over the years. He didn't speak about the team like just co-workers, I really felt that Gage had finally found a family."

"Have you known Gage long?"

"Twenty years. First time I met him, Alex and him showed up drunk at my sorority. The Sisters weren't happy at all to have two *SEALs* singing some nasty drinking song at the tops of their lungs on their porch."

"Did they leave the Navy together?"

He knew so little about Gage's past. All the stories that were told were as if Gage's life only started when he began working for Linus. Gage never mentioned family. He assumed he was like most of the Trenton Crew—they didn't have a biological family except for Linus and Pure's mom. He wanted to know everything about Gage, even the not so pretty parts and he wanted to know about the scars, what each represented.

"No, Gage left first, I think he wanted to settle in one spot. Alex only left a few years ago to spend more time with Cameron. To get to know his daughter again, he's taking all the blame because he talked me into letting her go. If he hadn't, then she'd...but if she hadn't been taken, Kray would've died in that basement. No one would have even cared. Cameron said he tried to take every punishment, used his body to shield hers. They bonded in that cell."

"He seemed like an amazing kid, and we'll do everything to make sure he gets all the help and love he needs."

"Did you want me to take over? You look ready to drop."

"Are you sure?"

"Yeah, I'd like to spend time with my soon-to-be kid. I always wanted to try for a son, but I couldn't have more after Cameron. My husband should be here soon. He was keeping everything at home from imploding with both bosses MIA. He's barely been holding on. Stanton needs to see Cameron to make him relax."

He eased his hand from Kray's and let Margo take his place. He was so tired he could barely walk a straight line, and when he made it back to the waiting room, Linus and Gage stood up.

"Is everything okay?" Gage asked.

"Both are sleeping. Kray crashed from exhaustion and Cameron had a panic attack, so they gave her something. Margo is going to sit with Kray and Alex is with Cameron. Everything cool here?"

"We have to stick around for a few days, but that's normal so they can check our stories." He watched as Linus handed Gage a key and a card in an small envelope. "Peaches picked up all our key cards for the hotel and keys for the rentals. Raul and Pure are already headed that way. Little and Livingston are making a food run. I'm going to stay here with Peaches while we sort out things. Why don't you and Gage go and crash, we have a lot of sleep to catch up on. Derrick," Linus said as he approached him.

"Yeah?"

"You did good. I'm so proud of you. You're a better man than that fucker who spawned you, and I hope you know that."

He closed his eyes against the tears as Linus leaned down slightly to press a kiss to his forehead. He was handed off to Gage, and they made their way to the exit after Gage told Linus to have Alex call him when he got a minute. The big man looked more exhausted than him but was probably still in a better position to drive. Gage opened the passenger door and helped him inside—he was too tired to talk or move. He just wanted to sleep for the next few days.

He must have dozed off as soon as they pulled out of the parking lot because the next thing he knew, Gage was saying his name. The man helped him out of his seat, and he leaned all his weight on Gage as they made it inside, up the elevator and to a room.

"Come on, boy, you need sleep."

He just nodded and let Gage strip him, and he was about to ask Gage to stay when firm lips pressed to his. "I'm gonna go shower, and I'll be back. Don't hog the bed."

"Yes, Daddy."

"You're not up to calling me Daddy right now."

He savored Gage's rough chuckle and turned on his side, snuggling under the covers. It didn't take him long to fall asleep, and he was so out of it that he barely moved when a naked Gage stretched out behind him.

GAGE HAD A STORY TO TELL

*A*rsenault eyes had been wide and filled with fear as him and Linus circled him where they had him knelt beside the shallow grave. They had both taken the kill shot, the barrel of their 9 millimeters pressed to the back of his head. They hadn't even flinched, just inhaled deep and squeezed the trigger as they exhaled. There was no guilt. No remorse. For him, he heard Kray begging for it to be him instead of Cameron. Kray deserved his revenge, and he didn't give a fuck what anyone had to say about it.

Out of everything he remembered of doing away with the dangerous animal Arsenault was, the conversation Linus and he had afterward stuck with him.

THE QUIET BETWEEN Linus and himself couldn't be called anything but oppressive. He knew neither of them regretted putting the fucker down, but they'd still taken a life. The tension slowly eased as they got into the rental car they'd stashed earlier. A silent decision was made that Kray wouldn't witness the act. They didn't want that memory to linger in

Kray's mind. It was time for the boy to move on, to start accepting his freedom and that he was no longer the captive of a sick, evil man.

"You okay, Gage?"

He took the time to think about his answer and looked deep inside himself to sense even the minute guilt. "I don't have any regrets, man. Kray and Cameron would never be safe with him still breathing." He glanced at Linus to catch just the hint of a nod.

"It was the right decision."

"It was. Linus, about Derrick..."

"You don't have to explain anything to me. If I'm honest, it was there for a long time. It was just something we'd never discussed. But, Gage, Derrick deserves to find his peace with who he is, and I don't know if you're able to fucking give him that."

"I'm not sure either, but I want a chance no matter how fucking unworthy I feel."

"Then take the chance, man, what do you have to lose?"

He had a lot to lose, and his biggest one was his heart. His love for his boy was inappropriate, and he'd always felt he should show mercy and leave his boy alone. After the operation, the lines he'd cross, it would be impossible to move on—to ignore what they'd started.

"I don't want to hurt him."

"Then don't."

It sounded so easy. It was more than an emotional scar he'd leave behind. His mind still played over the physical damage he could inflict. A simple moment of losing control and Derrick could bear the same bruises as Gage's mother. His fear held him back. Yet, could he truly give up the chance to make his boy his—to know a semblance of happiness in a life filled with pain and regret?

"Are you sure you...I don't know why, but I want your blessing in this."

"Gage, as much as I hate to think of my kids dating anyone, my son deserves to find love, and his heart is set on you. Just don't break him, Gage, you're a brother to me and out of everything in my life I've learned we protect family. Just think long and hard about this. If you *can see yourself loving my son, that his happiness is the most important thing to you, then don't fuck up your chance."*

They'd gone silent after that, making the long trek to the hospital to rejoin the team. He had a lot to think about and just hoped he'd make the right decision.

He PUT that night out of his mind as he snuggled his boy back to his chest and groaned as his boy's soft ass wiggled against his hard dick. Derrick still asleep turned over, and he smiled as Derrick slipped his thigh over his hip. He fisted his left hand in his boy's silky hair and tipped Derrick's head back enough to bring his mouth down on his boy's—the soft curves gave under his firmer lips. He reluctantly pushed his boy onto his back before things got out of hand. Before they went any farther, they needed to talk.

He wouldn't ask Derrick to consider being with him without the full truth. Last night on the way to the hospital, he'd asked Linus permission to ask Derrick out on a date. He respected his friend, and while Linus didn't know his complete backstory, he assumed Linus knew enough to make him wary of Gage being around his son. The death threat was expected, more so than the permission.

"Do you have a new one?"

Derrick's question confused him until fingertips traced the bandage on his forearm softly. He didn't ask when his boy had seen them. He'd slept shirtless beside Derrick, but he'd tried to wake up first and be ready for the day before Derrick's eyes even opened.

"You want to hear a story?"

"If you're in it, of course."

He settled in to snuggle while he could. He didn't know if he'd have another opportunity to hold his boy in his arms. If Derrick decided the risk wasn't worth it, then he'd have to respect

Derrick's wishes because the two of them had to trust each other completely. He wanted to take care of his boy. Make sure he was always happy, and before he could do that, Derrick had to hear it all.

"My father was in the Army...a meaner bastard had never been born. He had a philosophy on life where women needed to have their place and if they didn't learn it, then..." He paused as his throat started to close.

"You don't have to tell me. I don't have to know."

"Yes, you do, you have to know everything before I ask you on a date."

"Then, by all means, Daddy, tell away."

He brushed a kiss to his boy's forehead. "Brat." He laid his head on the pillow beside Derrick's. "The only happy times in my childhood were when he was deployed because as soon as he came home, it was hell in that house. When he was gone, my mother was happy and healthy. The Major, that's what he made me call him. His rank and nothing else. He made me watch him beat her. Said that I had to learn how to...I needed to learn how to train my wife. My mom was never obedient enough, so he had to hit her."

"Is she still alive?" Derrick slim fingers combed through the hair on his chest.

He shook his head. Sometimes her loss felt like it was only the day before. Always a festering wound that would never heal and maybe it wouldn't. Even though, as he grew older, he started to understand why she did it. "I came home one day, he was away, and she always met me in the kitchen. We'd have cookies...he didn't allow that kind of shit when he was home. She wasn't there. I searched the house, and I found her in the tub. I thought she was asleep. Come to find out Major had called and said he was on his way home that night. She'd talked to someone on base, and it got back to him, they joked about her cheating, but to him…she couldn't take another beating. She slit her wrists. To her, it was her only way to escape."

"I would have loved to have met her."

"She was beautiful and amazing. When it was just the two of us, she was so happy, but he didn't let her work. She didn't have a friend except for me. One day, not long before she died, she tried to explain to me what real love was, but I was too young to understand that.

"After she was gone something broke, I started having blackouts. Woke up in strange places covered in blood only to find out that I'd beaten the shit out of someone for looking at me. It kept happening, and alcohol became my best friend, which made the blackouts worse."

"Is that why you joined the Navy?"

"Yeah, I barely graduated, so it was my only way out, but I didn't want to serve anywhere near him. I wanted to be better. My life changed, and I learned to take control. Except I was always terrified." He hugged his boy to his chest and tried to figure out how to explain. What he had to say was easier when he'd practiced it in his head as he'd waited in the hospital. Voicing his thoughts was confusing, and he didn't feel he was explaining everything as clearly as he should.

"That you were him? Maybe you'd continue the cycle of abuse to your partner?"

He relaxed realizing his boy was getting it, and with Derrick's past, he needed this to be just right.

"That and I also knew early that I was different, and he would've killed me if he knew my first crush was a boy in my class. The internalized homophobia was killing me. I was as macho as I could get. I fucked women while on leave so no one would think differently. Alex knew though. He took me aside. I was drinking too much, partying too much and I was starting to lose it again."

"What changed?"

"Nothing, instead of thinking I'd beat my wife, it was now a husband. I couldn't allow myself to hurt anyone. That's when I decided quick anonymous fucks with no names exchanged was the way to go, then the worse thing in the fucking world happened."

"What?"

"I met a beautiful boy, with the most gorgeous brown eyes and sweetest smile. I wanted him more than anything in the world."

"Maybe he thought you were just as beautiful."

He chuckled as he traced his boy's lips with the tip of his index finger. "I doubt it. I'm an old man with wrinkles, gray hair and excessively grumpy."

"Grumpy can be sexy. Why do you do this?" Derrick wrapped soft hands around his wrist and lifted his arm.

He tensed as tender kisses stroked over the ridges of raised skin. "That's harder to explain. I needed a release...violence always gave me that. I wasn't as tense after my blackouts. Fucking wasn't an option...it wasn't the release I needed. Those people I took to bed did nothing for me. Some nights I barely kept my dick hard. The pain though, it was almost like the sting of my split and bruised knuckles. My broken ribs from the ones who were strong enough to fight back. It kept the monster at bay."

"There's so many."

"Daily ritual, same as someone who needs a cup of coffee to get their day started. I lined up my supplies at my kitchen table, cut, tended, and headed off to work. Alex is the only one who's sure of them, I know some people have caught sight of them over the years, but no one's ever said a word."

"Thank you for trusting me with your story. I know you're scared of hurting me, but the fact you've stayed away, I guess, trying to protect me proves I might be different and I'm not scared of you. I wanted to be yours since before I knew what that meant."

"Thorpe, he, I don't ever want to remind you of him. It's why I always stayed away. I always caught snippets of conversation, and when your name was mentioned, I listened closer. Wondered if you were dating or when you'd visit would that be the time you brought someone home."

"I won't say I didn't date. When I decided to take the job as a Deputy, I wanted to come home and have you see me as a man. Not your friend's annoying son."

"I don't want my boy to say he used other men to get ready for me."

"Would I say that? Would it earn me a spanking?"

"Of course, I'd get the bratty boy. What do you say I take you out on a date tonight? Since we're stuck here, I might as well get our first date out of the way."

"I'd love to, but first I want to go to the hospital and check on Kray and Cameron." Derrick turned his head to check the time on the digital clock beside the bed. "It's already noon."

"Damn, did anyone call? We didn't even wake up for food." He leaned over Derrick to grab their phones that he'd left on the nightstand. When he saw no messages or missed calls, no news was good news, right? He tensed above his boy as he felt a tug on the necklace with the key, and when he looked down, he found Derrick holding it between his teeth.

"Do I get to keep my collar?"

He shifted until he could rest between his boy's thighs and reminded himself his boy deserved some romance before they went further, but that didn't mean he couldn't make his boy feel less insecure.

"The day I walked into that shop, I bought a plain leather collar for the person who would be my partner, the person I assumed would be Pure, but this one"—he traced the warm metal with his fingertips—"this one, I bought for a dream, one I was never going to have. But when I looked at it, I could see him wearing it. This one I picked just for you. You can wear it as long as you want."

"I'm keeping it."

They kissed softly for long minutes, and he barely pulled away from Derrick before he said fuck dinner. He dropped one last quick kiss to his boy's smiling lips before he rolled from bed to head for the shower. He wouldn't fuck this up—he promised himself that, but that still didn't mean he wasn't terrified.

WAS NEEDING TO PUKE A BAD DATE OMEN?

Their first date became delayed by a day due to more questioning by the cops and a sketchy federal agent. Knowing the guy they'd taken down had friends in high places had made the Trenton Crew more paranoid than a tweaker on a four-day binge. Derrick was so ready to go home and leave this whole mess behind. Gage put on his fancy suit and did what he'd always done best, got the guys out of trouble. Hell, he'd almost believed the spin, and he'd been in on the operation.

Good news had traveled through the crew in the way of Cameron and Kray being released from the hospital. They'd given them a room all to themselves, and they'd spent hours locked inside. Raul had popped the lock a few times for the crew to check on them. Everything was arranged for them to go back to Alex's home. He knew Kray was waiting for the bottom to fall out and he'd end up back in a group home. The state therapist in charge of Kray's case said it would take time, and after meeting and spending time with Alex and Margo, he'd instantly known they were the perfect people for Kray.

Kray seemed overwhelmed by the kindness of strangers, particularly ones that said they wanted to adopt him. They'd discussed that Kray would live with Alex but also spend time with Margo. The tears the boy shed at the thought of having parents, even ones that lived separately, had been almost too much for the young man to handle. Cameron had been the only one who seemed able to calm him. Theirs was a bond formed in tragedy, and they couldn't imagine keeping them apart. They were the only two people who truly understood what they'd gone through and they needed each other.

Also, he had a bad feeling in his gut that told him this wasn't over. He tried to reassure himself that it was the culmination of weeks of stress. Although, his current problem was taking precedence, he needed to puke. A decade of waiting for Gage to see him and only hours away from their first date, he'd admit he was losing it a bit.

He was just starting to pour himself a cup of coffee when a knock sounded on the door. Everyone was at the hospital or cleaning up loose ends at the motel they'd used for their headquarters. Hunter was going through footage and editing out what didn't need to be seen or destroying the files altogether. He strode to the door, peeked through the peephole and frowned at the couple on the other side. He opened the door to Forester and Janette giving him warm smiles.

"Well, this is a surprise," he said and stepped back, "Please come in."

"Thank you," Forester replied and let his wife go first. "We were nervous about our reception."

"I will say, I'm a bit surprised to see you both."

He motioned toward the sitting area and observed them closely, Janette was offered a seat first and then Forester followed her down. The other man laid his arm across her lap, and Janette leaned into his strength. He might have thought the man was a bit sleazy to begin with, but the obvious love and devotion between the two people had eased his worries.

"I'm sure. We were headed into the city to attend an opera. My wife loves it, and I'll suffer through."

He chuckled as she bumped his arm with her shoulder and Forester gifted her with an adoring look.

"Would you like a cup of coffee?"

"No, no, this will be a quick visit, we just wanted to check on our mutual friend. I've heard that his rescue was successful."

"We got him out, and our friend's daughter was with him, but they both have a long road ahead."

"That's one of the reasons we came to see you. Is he being taken care of, offered a place to recuperate? Janette and I wanted to offer our home and time if he needed a place."

"I don't know how that would go over."

As great as the offer was, he didn't know how Kray would react to being reminded of his life before. The couple in front of him seemed nice enough, but with everything about the operation, he wasn't willing to react by his gut instinct alone.

"That was also a concern. As much as we tried to show him kindness, it was difficult."

"Alex is petitioning for guardianship, and we have a lawyer helping, once that comes through, he'll be adopted by Alex."

"You are an amazing group of people. Is Hayden around?"

Okay, he didn't know if it was jealousy or suspicion, but he didn't like the too handsome man asking about Gage. Rough edges or not, Gage had this bearing of elegance around him. The man was able to blend into any scene, morph into a dangerous bail enforcement agent or hold his own with sickeningly rich and elegant men. Maybe that was part of why he was ill. He still wasn't sure he'd grown up enough to be the man Gage needed. He'd lived on his own for a long time, took care of himself and his brother, he was independent and assumed he was good at his job. Despite wanting to be his Daddy's boy, he still wanted Gage to see him as a man.

"No, he's off taking care of business. He's kicking public relation ass at the moment."

"Well, please let him know that we stopped by to congratulate everyone on their success. You and him are welcome to visit at any time. Although, I'm a stickler for tradition, Janette and I have decided our events have run their course. It would be wonderful though to get to know you and Hayden on a more even footing."

"I'll let Gage know." He leaned forward to take the card Forester handed him. He studied the elegant face of the business card.

"Also, in my former life I was a judge, if Trenton ever requires a bit of legal help, I offer my assistance and I owe you and your team a debt of gratitude for removing Kray from the situation. I'll forever bear the guilt of not seeing through Arsenault's act sooner. While I didn't respect the man, I didn't believe him capable of what he'd done."

"Monsters aren't always easy to spot. Some of them have a lot of practice blending, and I'm sure you would've stepped in if you'd sensed something as severe as what Kray went through. My biological father was eviler than we'd even anticipated, so I know how easy it is to not see everything even when it's right in your face."

Forester gave him a grateful smile, then stood and helped his wife to her feet. The goodbyes were quick, and he was thankful that Gage hadn't returned while they were there. When they'd been at Forester's estate, he hadn't missed the appreciation and attraction Forester seemed to have for Gage. That was fine for everyone else, it worked well for his dads, but he'd never be able to share Gage. He'd waited too fucking long to be where he was, and Forester made him insecure.

"Derrick, why aren't you ready?" Peaches breezed into the suite in her civilian clothes with all her tattoos on display, and the bells weaved into her hair tinkling with every step.

He remembered when Kray had seen her the first time out of

her expensive pantsuit and professional bun. The boy had been fascinated, and when she'd leaned close to him, she'd handed Kray a handful of silvery blonde, belled braids. The sound of them seemed to calm Kray so they'd ran out and got him windchimes that made a sound close to the bells. They'd hung them in his and Cameron's room, a fan gently blowing a breeze through them.

"We had guests. I need to puke."

"No you don't. It's a date, and you've known Gage forever. You'll do great."

"What if the longer he's around me, the less he likes me?"

"Quit freaking the fuck out. If he doesn't like you that's his shit, ain't got nothing to do with you. Now go get ready, I'm going to call my sexy husband and have him talk dirty to me. We never go a day without sex, lots and lots of sweaty, nasty..."

He ran with Peaches laughing her ass off hysterically behind him. When they'd brought him into the Crews and he got to know them all, their craziness had nothing on that of the Matriarchs of the Crews, Peaches and Lily. Peaches didn't take shit from anyone, and he'd seen her go toe-to-toe with Thorpe over the years. When she threatened to bury him, he'd had no doubt she would've, and he'd been terrified to approach her after Thorpe shot her the night that he tried to take out the Crews at Brawlers.

He quickly got ready, took extra time in the shower and fussing over his appearance. He'd thought about trimming his pubes, but he wasn't exactly prepared for a date night. He screamed as he stormed out of the bathroom, naked and walked quickly to the bed to put on the clothes he'd laid out. At least he had some nice things they'd packed for being at Forester's.

"If I was less of a gentleman, I'd say fuck the date."

Gage's low, guttural tone had him spinning with his boxer briefs in his hand to find Gage leaned against the door. The way the man ran his gaze over Derrick's body made him nervous.

He'd always been on the slimmer side, strong but lean, and his ass was what some would call mushy. He had to admit most of his weight had always been on his ass.

He tried not to retreat as Gage pushed his big body away from the door, and with a lazy swagger, made his way to him.

"I love that you're wearing this," Gage whispered as he ran his fingers along the chain.

The possessiveness in the man's gaze caused his body to flush with heat. All the years he'd imagined they'd be together didn't prepare him. Being naked while Gage was fully clothed was erotic, as if he were at the man's mercy. He'd submit to anything the man asked of him.

"I'm scared." He twisted his upper body slightly to drop his underwear to the bed and turned back to face Gage.

"Of me?"

"No, well, in a way. I'm terrified you won't like the man I am."

"I adore the man you are. Yes, I've avoided being around you." Gage lowered his head until his mouth was just over his. "You were so much temptation. I wanted to play with my boy. Love on you, but scared I'd hurt you. I wouldn't do that for the world."

His back arched at the rough caress of Gage's hands from his collarbones down his chest until Gage's arms twined around his waist. He was pulled flush to the bigger man. There wasn't much difference in their heights, but Gage's body was bulkier and broader than his. He squeaked as Gage grabbed his ass and squeezed the soft curves.

"You rubbing this ass against my cock every night was fucking torture."

"I still remember what you felt like inside me."

"I'm sorry for that. I wouldn't...I lost control."

"I didn't mind. I never bottomed before...that was supposed to be yours."

"And it will be, after I take my beautiful boy on our first date."

He tensed as Gage dropped to his knees in front of him,

reaching behind him to grab the underwear he'd discarded. Gage slowly lifted one foot then the other and slid the fabric up his legs. His dick went instantly hard as Gage pressed his face into his cotton-covered crotch. "Daddy." It slipped so easily from his mouth as Gage gently nipped his cock through his underwear.

Being dressed by Gage was one of the biggest turns-ons he'd ever experienced. He didn't understand how that was possible. Gage surged to his feet to slip the dress shirt onto his arms, lovingly brushing his stomach and chest with each button the man secured. His breaths were coming out in quick pants until he felt lightheaded.

"Do you want to make your Daddy happy?" Gage asked between soft, teasing kisses, the smallest nips to the curves.

He nodded his head, and as their mouths brushed together, he watched Gage from under his lowered lashes. All Gage had to do was ask, and he was helpless to deny him. The feelings he'd had for Gage, that first stirring when he was seventeen and had seen the man for the first time, was mild compared to almost a decade later. Infatuation morphing into love, he loved the man for his flaws and perseverance. Loved him for the things the man probably hated about himself.

"Then have dinner with me, tell me everything about you and don't leave out the smallest detail. Then when we come back to the room, you just let me love on you. I've dreamed of taking you hard and fast, wherever I saw fit, but tonight, our first time together, I just want to memorize every gasp and shiver. Can you do that for me?"

"Yes."

"Yes, what?"

"Yes, Daddy."

"I'll never tire of you saying that one word all breathless and needy."

When he thought Gage would kiss him again, the man just took his hand and led him from the room. On the drive over, he told Gage every detail of his life while he was away. Confessed his hopes and dreams as Gage held his hand, only releasing it when they arrived at the restaurant and did just as Gage asked all through dinner as the tension of what was to come built. He was nervous and ready at the same time, he wanted to know what it was to be loved.

GAGE NEEDED TO MAKE THIS GOOD...
NO HE NEED IT TO BE AMAZING

*T*hey spent hours at dinner, exchanging stories and for the first time in his life, he'd felt relaxed. Almost as if the monster no longer lurked beneath the surface. He touched and kissed his boy whenever he wanted. Studied the curve of his boy's shy smile as Derrick told him about all he'd missed while he'd tried to be noble and protect his boy from him.

He needed his boy—it wasn't something as weak as a simple want. The signs had always been there no matter how much he tried to deny it. When they returned to the suite after dinner, he didn't pause as he led his boy through the room. He rolled his eyes as all his friends grinned and told them goodnight. Derrick had steadily grown more nervous on the trip back, and he knew his boy did know what would happen between them. Well, he was about to shock Derrick.

This moment had taken too long to come, and he wasn't in any mood to rush it. They had plenty of time for more later. As he'd told Derrick before they left for dinner, he was going to love on him. It was an experience he'd never had with anyone else. He wasn't in the mood to just get off. He kicked the door closed behind them and watched Derrick's shoulders tense as the lock clicked into place.

"Turn around."

Derrick only hesitated a few seconds then his boy pivoted to face him. The corner of his mouth pulled into a smirk as he took one step, then another, slowly stalking him and he sensed his boy wanted to retreat. He was proud when Derrick held his ground. He needed his boy right there with him; their need mutual. All the teasing kisses had intensified his need, and he finally captured his boy's lips in a slow deep kiss. Derrick moaned and tipped his head back, asking for more, and he gave his boy everything he needed. As he picked apart the buttons on Derrick's dress shirt, he walked his boy back to the bed.

"Have you touched yourself thinking about me, boy?"

"Yes, Daddy."

He nipped Derrick's bottom lip sharply and loved his needy whimper. He stripped his boy of his shirt, then slowly he removed the rest of Derrick's clothes and lowered to his knees. He brushed his lips across and nipped every inch of skin he exposed until Derrick's body glistened with sweat, his boy's pretty cock standing hard for him.

He drew out every second, minute, an hour could've passed, and he refused to leave a single spot of Derrick unloved, when he was done with the front, with his hands on his boy's hips, he turned him. "Bend over, Daddy wants to see what's his." He loved the lush curves in his hands as he palmed them, then parted them to see his boy's freshly shaved hole. "Were you thinking of me playing with your hole tonight?"

Gage hummed as he felt his boy bend over farther to rest his cheek on the bed. "Daddy, please."

"I'll give you just what you need, but when I'm ready." He brought his left hand back and then forward to watch that sexy jiggle of his boy's fuzzy ass cheek. The yelp was music to his ears. It was deeper and needier than the one when he'd spanked him at the estate. He parted his boy's cheeks again and pushed his face between them, licking over the tight, wrinkled skin. His boy's thighs shook, and he pushed his arms between them to spread his hands over the silky plane of his boy's belly to hold him up.

Derrick's scent, taste—he could feast on his boy's ass all night. He stiffened his tongue and pushed forward, the clench and give caused him to growl. Then the rumble in his chest deepened when slender fingers gripped his hair and Derrick began to move his hips riding the tip of his tongue. He hadn't given his boy permission to touch him or move, so he punished him by retreating and then giving him several smacks until his boy tried to get away.

He surged to his feet. "Don't move, you don't touch Daddy without his permission. I give you what you need when I'm ready not when you think you are." He leaned over and grabbed the back of his boy's collar and used it to control him, straightening his boy and then forced him to his knees. He released the chain and stepped backward. He lazily moved around the room removing his jacket, shirt, and made no attempt to speak to his boy again.

His boy was sexy there on his knees, trembling from head to toe and breathing too fast. Once he was naked, he slid open the dresser drawer and took out the condoms and lube he'd bought the day before. He spared his boy a short glance. He arranged the pillows and threw the covers to the foot of the bed, then placed the supplies on the bed. His cock was hard and leaking precum. He couldn't remember the last time he was more turned on, no one but his boy affected him like that.

He sat cross-legged on the bed. "Come here, boy." He didn't take his gaze from his boy's flushed face, cheeks the prettiest shade of pink and Derrick crawled to him. Derrick sat on his thighs, and he positioned his boy's legs around his waist. They both moaned as their bodies came together.

"Drape your arms over my shoulders." As Derrick did as he

asked, he turned his head to brush his mouth to the lean muscles of Derrick's upper arm, one then the other. "Did you think I would just bend you over and fuck you?"

"I-I didn't know."

He felt the movement and shape of Derrick's mouth as he answered. They shared kisses, and he traced the lines of his boy with just the tips of his fingers. Savoring the texture of chill bumps moving in their wake. Sweat misted his own body, and his cock pulsed where it rested next to his boy's. His touches to his boy's hole were light and nowhere near what his boy begged for. "Shh, boy, those sweet little cries are for my ears only, do you understand Daddy?"

"But I can't be quiet, too much."

"When we get home and you're in my bed, you can scream all you want, but your pleasure is only mine. I hated sharing you at the estate. I'm sorry I had to do that." As much as he loved the freedom to touch his boy at the estate—a chance to be selfish—he hadn't liked others seeing the beautiful boy that belonged to him.

"It's okay."

"No, it's not, it wasn't respectful to Daddy's good boy." He picked up the lube, and the top clicked as he opened it, then slicked his finger and set it aside. "When I start playing with your hole, you push out."

The position had Derrick spread perfectly for him to massage the slick around his boy's hole. His boy's head fell back, and his breathing increased as he slowly worked from one finger to three. His own cock was pulsing to the point of pain, his balls aching with the need to fuck his boy. His boy kept repeating Daddy, begging for more and every time his boy tried to fuck himself onto his fingers, he'd smacked his ass in warning. He slipped from his boy's well-stretched hole.

He was quickly moving to dangerous territory, but he wanted his boy's mouth on his dick. "Suck Daddy's dick, boy." He laid back and stretched out his legs. "Fuck," he growled as his boy swallowed his cock. His boy's lips stretched wide around the girth of his dick. He combed his fingers through silky hair and then gripped it in a brutal grip as he taught his boy what he liked. His stomach sucked in with pleasure as his boy whimpered and hummed. "Daddy's naughty boy likes sucking dick." He held his boy's face to his crotch and thrust upward forcing his cock to the back of his boy's throat. He repeated that several times until he jerked his boy from his cock. He tugged his boy up his body by his hair and took his mouth, pushed his tongue inside.

He lost all control as he manhandled his boy onto his hands and knees. His chest hurt with his attempts to breathe, and he got himself ready, rolling on the condom and added more lube. He stiffened and tightened his jaw as he placed his fat cockhead to his boy's ass. His boy's hole gave easily, and it was pleasure and agony. He grabbed the back of the collar and pulled, his boy's body arched, and he thrust fast—his hips slapping against his boy's ass, then pulled back in slow motion.

"More, Daddy, please."

He didn't think twice about giving in, and he fucked his boy's hole brutally, stared down at where his cock disappeared and reappeared over and over. His body came down on Derrick's, his legs straddling his boy's and he had his hand around the front of Derrick's slender throat, squeezing enough to restrict but not cut off his boy's breathing. He rutted against Derrick's ass, felt the clench of his boy's hole every time he pulled out.

"Shit, boy, you were made for Daddy's cock. You like your Daddy fucking you, owning you?"

"Yes, Daddy, I'm gonna..." Derrick's broke off with a deep groan as his boy started riding his cock and rubbing against the bed.

"Oh yeah, come on Daddy's cock. Daddy's boy always comes first." Fire moved through his veins and his muscles tensed to the point of pain. Then he squeezed his boy's throat harder and lowered his head to sink his teeth into Derrick's shoulder. He slammed his free hand over his boy's mouth as the agonized scream nearly alerted everyone to his release. His thrusts became shorter and more grinding against his boy's plump ass, then his cheeks clenched, and he emptied every drop of cum into the latex.

As he came back to himself, he felt the wetness of tears on his hand, and he turned Derrick's face to his and kissed the salty drops from his red face. He rolled them to the side to get his boy out of the wet spot, held the base of the condom and eased reluctantly from his boy's still contracting hole. Derrick was suddenly on his side with his arms wrapped around him, his boy was shaking and letting out these soft sobs.

"Hey, boy, what's wrong?"

Derrick was hiding his face against his chest, and he couldn't have that. He might get rough, but he'd never hurt his boy, and he needed his boy to trust him to tell him what was wrong.

"Derrick, don't make me repeat myself. Was it too much?"

"It was perfect." Derrick tilted his head back, and Gage raised his hand to stroke the hair from Derrick's face.

"Then why the tears?"

"Is it always that intense?"

"Your pleasure is important to me, and I wanted you to feel how much you mean to me." He stroked and soothed until his boy calmed, his boy going limp beside him, but Derrick hadn't fallen asleep. He slowly removed himself from Derrick's embrace to go clean up and dispose of the condom. He stared into the mirror and didn't recognize the relaxed and satisfied man staring back at him. He didn't want to leave his boy alone long, so he went to the bathroom, washed his cock and balls with a warm rag, then grabbed a clean one for his boy.

By the time he returned with a warm wet rag, Derrick was spread out on the bed, arms and legs splayed wide. He'd noticed when his boy was alone in bed the boy sprawled in all directions. He took care of tending to his boy and slipped into bed. They shared caresses and kisses, talked in whispered tones until they both grew tired. His boy had been well worth the wait, and he'd never regret making Derrick his.

THE LIFE DERRICK ALWAYS WANTED

They'd arrived back in Powers a few days before, and he started settling back into his everyday life. The cloud of suspicion still hung over their heads, but without Arsenault's body, they had no cause to keep them in New York longer. Arsenault's men couldn't say the man was dead because they weren't conscious when the bastard disappeared. No body, no crime and they sure as hell weren't offering to help.

He looked up from his desk to catch Wren walking through the front door. Wren had tried to stick to days, but his body didn't function on a day shift.

"The joys of paperwork."

He snorted as Wren gave him a quick kiss on the top of his head as the other man headed to his desk. "You're late."

"I think the place is still standing and, well, I don't like getting out bed with my men still in it."

"Ugh, don't be gross.

"Why are you still here? Your shift ended fifteen minutes ago and the boss ain't here."

He signed the report on the one traffic stop he'd made that day and smiled at how laidback Powers had become. He remembered the way it was before Pelter had taken over. Pelter may not be as strict in his policing as he'd once been, but the man didn't let the bullshit run rampant as Thorpe allowed in the decades as Sheriff.

"We're back to the real world."

"And what's wrong with the real world?" Wren asked as the man perched on the corner of his desk.

He pretended to read the report again because voicing his problem was going to make him sound like an idiot. Whining in his head was one thing, making it real by speaking it was another. Gage and him had a week of dates and learning about each other, talked about childhoods and dreams. They had sex only the once because the days were filled with interrogations and working together to make sure Cameron and Kray were getting everything they needed.

Although, they'd slept in the same bed every night, sharing kisses and everything couples normally shared. All that ended the moment they'd returned.

"Son?"

Wren was a sneaky fucker, the fads had a way of saying that one word, and it made him want to confess everything. A single syllable which carried every dream he'd had of a parent who had cared about him—a parent who worried if he was safe and warm. His own mother hadn't spoken to him since the night the Trenton team had taken him through his bedroom window. The memory of Wren's expression as he'd looked down on Pride's bruised cheek, a look of rage and love at first sight. He'd struggled with his upbringing for years until he'd accepted that he wasn't at fault for the lack of love from his biological parents.

"Did I ever tell you how much being a part of your family meant to me? The first night was the safest I'd ever felt."

"We loved you being there. Linus shocked me when he told me he'd petitioned for custody because he liked seeing me so happy. You and Pride made our little family complete. Now, are you going to tell me what you meant?"

He'd analyzed every scenario since coming home. Gage was busy as all the Trenton guys were settling back in, trying to knock jobs off the board since Cameron had taken precedence. He didn't want to appear needy with one date and a single fuck under their belt.

"I'm wondering if the job made"—he took a deep breath and exhaled slowly—"I mean, I'm wondering if there is a me and Gage now that the operation is over. It pushed us together and maybe what we started isn't as deep as I'd hoped."

"You think you had a little fun on the job and now you're back to your real lives. Adults have to work at relationships, it's not easy or like those romance novels where it's all tied up in a nice bow at the end. It's dirty, hard work, but more than worth the effort. I'm not saying I completely approve of you and Gage—"

"What's wrong with me and Gage?"

"He's not…I'm not trying to be insulting…but he's kinda cold and standoffish. All the time I've known him, I haven't once seen him with anyone or heard him mention dating at all."

The story Gage told him played through his head, and it explained the way Gage acted—how he perceived himself—but it wasn't his place to say anything. The man had trusted him with pieces of his life he hadn't shared with anyone. He couldn't fathom what it was like for Gage to be that young and find his mother dead, then be trapped with her tormentor until Gage turned eighteen. He didn't see the monster that Gage claimed himself to be.

"He has his reasons."

"Fair enough. Have you seen him since you've been back? Linus has been working long hours, and I heard Gage took an assignment off the board. Linus seemed concerned by that."

He frowned, Gage had sent him texts, but he hadn't mentioned going on a job. The man had pulled out of the field a few years ago, slowly transitioning to strictly PR. He had gone along with Peaches when Little had gone undercover at a rehab facility and undergone experiments, and he even took part in breaking Little out. Other than that, Gage didn't do fieldwork. He worried over why Gage hadn't told him.

"We've exchanged messages, but I hadn't been working here long before I was asked to help with finding Cameron. I wanted to focus on this, and I know Trenton is in catch up hell."

He didn't want to admit he was acting like a kid with his first crush. The one thought running through his head was that if he went to Gage, what they shared would be different. That the connection they had working together wouldn't exist anymore. He hated the insecurity.

"Yeah, their board is insane."

"How long is Gage gone for?"

"Him, Liv and Pure left out last night, probably be a few days or so."

"Raul didn't go?"

"Little's on another job and Raul was asked to test a security system. Raul wasn't happy about it."

"I'm sure." Raul and Pure had automatically become partners. Raul acted as Pure's spotter or whatever. They never went on different jobs.

"Go home, get your shit together, then be the man I know you are and get your man. People might not think so, but I always believed that the struggle to maintain love was always more powerful than all the pieces fitting together perfectly."

"Thanks. I know I'm being an idiot. It's just that it's been nothing but stress for weeks. I should've known I'd crash and burn at some point."

"You need rest to clear your head."

He got up from his desk and hugged Wren before grabbing his backpack. He had to get out of his head, maybe actually go do something. To be honest, he hadn't really made Powers his home again. When he exited the building, he turned the opposite direction from home and went to hit the funky side street that was home to Decadence Bakery, Twirled World, Well Loved Thrift and others. They were places he wasn't allowed to go growing up, and he liked the variety of characters he found there.

If Gage was out of town, he couldn't take care of whatever problem was between them until the man returned. As soon as he turned onto the street laughter rang out from the cute pink haired Trevor and Grace was throwing things at him.

"Don't be an asshole," Grace said through her laughter. She was wearing a dress that looked like it was made in the fifties with a belt cinched around her thick waist that made her hips look wider. She had her hair in elegant rolls. She'd moved there a few years ago after being long-distance friends with Harper who owned the local bookstore, and he adored her quirkiness.

"I wasn't. I gave amazing advice." Trevor danced his chunky form around her as he shoved a phone in her face and she elbowed him away.

"My dating life is none of your concern."

"Just swipe one, have some sexy Daddy rock your granny panties."

"I'm firing you."

"Um, I don't technically work here."

"Am I interrupting?" he asked as he stuck out his cheek and Trevor gave him a loud kiss. Trevor had relocated there a few months ago after what he'd heard was a nasty divorce. The kid didn't look old enough to be out of high school much less recently divorced.

"I'm trying to get Grace to go on a date with this sinfully sexy Silver Fox that looks like he's rocking a concealed weapon. She's being stubborn."

"Aw, come on, Grace, he's"—he peeked at the screen—"um, wow, if you don't I will."

"An ally! Yes!"

"I'm just settling in. I have no time for—" She paused as Trevor waved the phone in front of her again. "You know I don't date. Now, come on, we're all meeting up at the diner for dinner."

In the span of a few seconds, he was ordered to eat with them, and he helped push the clothes racks back into the shop. He needed a distraction, and the perfect one had come up. He needed to spend time with friends and clear his head. Tomorrow he'd figure out how to get his Daddy back because not having him wasn't an option. As had become his nervous habit, he fingered the lock and brought it to his lips.

"Someone is wearing a very nice new accessory, and I require details."

Trevor looped his arms around him and asked a million questions, he avoided most, but at least he didn't mention names. Trevor was sweet, but the boy spread gossip the quickest in Powers. There were some things he wasn't quite ready to share just yet. He was so close to having the life he always wanted.

ARE YOU TRYING TO GET YOURSELF KILLED!

"*D*own, down, down, Bail Enforcement!" *They breached the front door with their weapons out, and hands went up, bodies couldn't hit the floor fast enough. This was his third fugitive capture in the past week. They cleared the room, checked the others as Linus used zip ties to restrain their mark.*

He entered a bedroom, and a few feet into the room, the press of a barrel at the base of his skull froze him in place. It wasn't the gun on him—it was the click of a misfire that had his heart stopping. His body reacted before his brain could, and he spun disarming the kid because that's what it was. He looked no more than early teens. The hatred in his eyes was far older than his years. He held the kid's gun beside him as he slid his into his holster. He rolled the kid to his back and placed his knee between the kid's shoulder blades.

"Clear," he yelled and noticed Pure glaring down at him. "What?"

"Are you trying to get yourself killed?" Pure growled low.

"What the fuck are you—"

"You didn't check your fucking blind spots. This isn't your first rookie mistake this week."

"Drop it." He handed the weapon over, then zip tied the thin wrists of his almost murderer.

. . .

THE SCENE from earlier in the night kept playing on repeat in his head. The adrenaline was still pumping even hours later, and he was in for a crash. He slammed back his fourth shot as he felt the eyes of his teammates and friends on him. No one had mentioned anything yet, but he knew it was coming and he was prepared. His thoughts were fucked up since he'd returned home from the operation.

Everyone was safe, Cameron was home, and Kray was learning to live with a family. Things weren't going smoothly, but that was expected. Everyone around him was back to normal or attempting to get there. Except his headspace was fucked beyond belief.

"Hello, Daddy."

He turned his head as a seductive male voice said close to his ear, then he had some stranger wrapped around him. The body was nothing like his boy's, and he didn't like the little bastard taking liberties. He downed another shot, and his body was starting to warm, his thinking grew fuzzy. Every night for seven days he'd tried to drink the lingering doubt away.

"Boy, fuck off, some other Daddy would be more than happy to take you on, but it ain't me."

"How do you know, I could definitely make it worth your—" Each word the guy spoke, his hand moved lower, and Gage was reaching the point of being pissed. Just as he was about to grab the guy's wrist, the body against him disappeared, and the broad back of Pure blocked his line of sight.

"I think the man said get lost." Pure's voice was filled with rage.

There was one certainty in life that he could guarantee, and that was Pure never got angry easily. Pure had to be pushed into a corner before he lashed out. He had a feeling he wasn't the only one with shit on his mind. He figured Pure had it handled so he started to ask for another, and the glass was taken from him and turned over.

"That's the end." Pure's tone didn't invite protest. "Want to talk it out because I'm not going anywhere until you do."

"What's there to talk about?"

"One, you don't drink, and you've been drunk seven nights in a row. Two, your rooms have been next to mine, and you've woken me up screaming. Three, for a man in love, you're awful fucking miserable."

"It's none of your fucking—"

"Wrong, if you're going to keep doing fieldwork, it's very much *my* business. Especially when you get one of my friends or my spotter killed. I'll take the kill shot with no remorse."

Pure wasn't lying, he could see it in the man's gaze, and the almost pretty man was downright vicious. In the years he'd known him, he'd never once seen Pure's finger hesitate on the trigger. All snipers needed a ruthless calm about them. It wasn't easy to know you took lives for a living. It didn't matter that Pure shot more non-lethal rounds than real ones lately, he knew the young man had no qualms, and he never wanted to be in Pure's crosshairs.

"I don't know what fucked up shit you got going in your head, but you're not leaving until you talk it out."

Pure ordered them both coffee, and without protest, he followed Pure to a booth in a quieter corner of the bar he'd found just down the street from their motel. He wearily fell into one side of the booth. His buzz was slowly fading, and he placed his elbows on the table, then scrubbed his hands over his face. He felt old and tired. This was one of the reasons he'd given up fieldwork—it wasn't in him anymore to be knocking down doors.

"Is this about Derrick? Because I thought things were going good…maybe not what I'd call normal, but you people and your obsession with your boys is weird."

He roughly chuckled behind his hands and smiled for the first time in days. "You might like having a Daddy."

"I'll pass, thank you very much. I want a husband and a houseful of kids one day."

He dropped his hands from his face and stared at Pure, the fact the man wasn't looking at him told him Pure was embarrassed he'd admitted his dream. "Kids?" Yeah, Pure was the type you'd see coming down the street and cross the road to avoid passing him, but the real Pure was sweet and shy, and more than a little repressed.

"Yeah, what's wrong with kids? They're sweet and fun, their love unconditional."

"Having a Daddy doesn't mean you can't have a loving husband and all your kids. Daddies just want to make sure their boys are happy and safe, want them to trust enough to know that they know what's best. Some men need more...guidance, support, Pure, some need comfort. There's nothing shameful about it."

Something flickered in Pure's gaze, but while they were friends, they'd never been particularly close, and he knew his explanation didn't satisfy something in Pure. He wanted to demand answers, ask if there was someone that needed to be taught a lesson. Except it wasn't his place, Pure didn't belong to him. What he did know of the man, he felt very bad about Raul's chances with Pure.

"We're not talking about me."

"My old man was one mean sonofabitch. He beat the fuck out of my mom every day he was home from deployment. Said women needed to be taught their place. She had no friends. No family left. I fucking hated him. Some guys saw my mom talking with some guy in the grocery store, probably just telling him where the toilet paper was. My dad's friends started joking that his old lady had a younger man on the side. He called her from training when he found out, and she killed herself an hour later. I'm fucking terrified I'm him."

"Joker does just fine and Dem ain't scared of him."

Joker had been tortured by his old man for years until one day he blacked out and beat the fucker to death. They'd put sixteen-year-old Joker in prison with grown men, and that's where the final step to becoming a monster began. Evil men were made, conditioned and hardened to violence.

"I blackout and—I've come to with men at my feet that I'd attacked for no reason. When we…we were on assignment, I was so focused on the job I had to do. On finding Cameron and rescuing Kray I had no chance to actually think about being with Derrick and what a normal, everyday life would be."

"So you don't want to be with him?"

"That's not the problem, I want him more now, and that's the scary part. It's not want or need, it's possessiveness. After we got home and I was away from him for a day, all my doubts and fears came back. I couldn't survive if I hurt him."

"Then you're different. If you didn't care about hurting him then I'd say leave him alone, but you do, and that makes all the difference. You may consider him your…boy, but Derrick is still a man who deserves to have his wishes respected."

"But what if?"

He nearly flinched back as Pure stretched his arm across the expanse of the table and dug out the key hanging around his neck. "You gave him a symbol of promise. A physical vow of your care and affection, isn't it cruel to make him wear your ownership and not claim the right to it?"

"For someone who doesn't like the dynamic you sure as fuck get it."

He smiled at Pure's rough snort, and Pure dropped the key, then picked up his coffee with both hands.

"I've been with the Trenton team a long time and the rest of the Crews...you learn stuff. Beyond the bullshit answers, what's your real problem?"

He slumped back onto the bench seat and pushed through the terror to what it masked. It was there hidden in the darkness, something that if he didn't name it that it wouldn't be true. What would happen if everyone knew the truth of what really held him back?

"What if the man I love, the only person I ever wanted to claim, thinks a razor and a tub of bloody water is his only way out?" He shoved his long sleeves up his arms and exposed his secret. The bandages that had covered fresh wounds tangled in the cotton and caught in the hollow of his elbow. "I've imagined a thousand times what her final thought was, the last thing she felt, and it fucking horrifies me that she thought this was her only way to happiness."

"You're thinking about it wrong. For someone who never had a choice in life, what's the one thing that you have the ultimate control over?"

"What?"

"The power to escape, death to her may have been taking her life back the only way she knew, and it was a shitty thing to do to you as a kid, but some people just want to die on their terms. He'd isolated her until she knew nothing else but the inside of her prison. Her death was quick, what death would your old man have given her?"

I'M SORRY, BOY

Two weeks, three hours, twenty-seven minutes and some odd seconds elapsed since Gage had left town for what Derrick had thought was a single job. He made plans about getting his Daddy back, forced himself to forget about it, then devised more plans. He didn't know what to do with himself. While he'd thought they'd had a great start, a little unconventional but they were members of four insane Crews and it was par for the course. He'd dreaded his days off and had even offered to pull overtime, but a booming metropolis Powers County wasn't. While on the large side for a town with the recent growth of new business and residents, it was one of the safest places to live.

While he stood at the counter with his ankles crossed, he spooned ice cream into his mouth from the carton. A real meal would be the adult thing to do, but he didn't feel like cooking and Heidi's Diner was packed on Friday nights.

His phone rang, and he debated a minute whether to ignore it or not, but he couldn't, in case it was an emergency. He picked it up without checking the display and connected the call.

"Come outside," Gage ordered before he even had a chance to say hello and then the call was disconnected.

He set his phone and ice cream aside and strode towards the front door. When he opened it, he found Gage seated sideways on his motorcycle, painted with a hypnotic blend of purples and reds, and the elegant chrome stood out starkly against the dark paint. Gage wore a short-sleeved shirt that hugged his muscular upper body and his jeans hinted at the strength of his legs. His man's normally neatly styled hair was mussed from the wind.

"You know you're supposed to wear a helmet." He fussed as he approached Gage and nearly stumbled as the man gave him a sexy smirk. That was new.

"More dangerous things in life than riding without one, I like to live dangerously."

"Is that so, and what are these more dangerous things of which you speak?" He stopped a few feet from Gage to keep himself from touching him. "Did you come to get your collar back?" As he asked the question, he raised his hand to the item in question. While Gage had sent texts over the time the man was away, they became fewer and shorter. It was the only reason he could think of for Gage to be there.

"No, that will always belong to you because you belong to me."

"You have a funny way of showing it."

"Boy, come here," Gage ordered as he stood up.

Gage held out his arms, and he was too weak to resist, he couldn't think of anywhere he'd rather be no matter how brief. He held tight to Gage and sighed as he inhaled the sandalwood scent that always seemed to cling to the man. It wasn't overpowering, it smelled like home, and he'd missed it. He felt the brush of Gage's lips to his temple.

"I wanted you too much. I thought it would be safer to talk out here."

"What did you want to talk about?" He stepped back with an

uneasy feeling. Gage wanted him, but the man's past still held too strongly to his psyche. The what-ifs of what could happen if he ever lost his temper. He respected Gage's limits and knew after Gage had told him the story that starting a relationship with the man wouldn't be easy. The man he needed had darker demons to slay than he did.

"I told you a half story. I left out a part of why I cut."

"And?"

"I wanted to know what my mother experienced in her last moments. Why it was easier to slit her wrists than it was to fight for her freedom? I know the sting of the razor, the first moment of hesitation, and then the release as the first drop escapes. I've had nightmares where you're in that tub and not her...that you were so fearful. I know, I know." Gage paced with irritation. "Intellectually I know, I'm not him. But I see it, the feelings all too real. In my nightmares, I'm him, and I'm making an appointment with Kieran as soon as I can. I have to work through it."

"Until you do, what's that mean for us?"

"Dates. Learning to be a team, I don't think we did too badly while working together. This will be all new for me, I've never dated before, and we don't have to be on guard. I'm sorry, boy, but I had to get my head around it before I came to you. The more days that went by, the more insecure I got that you'd still want me. I'm no prize, and I take the Daddy thing to the extreme sometimes."

"I don't mind the Daddy thing, twenty-four-seven or just in the bedroom is fine with me."

"After you went away to college—"

Gage paused as if he were looking for the right words. "Don't make it pretty, Daddy, I'd prefer if you were honest."

"Your first trip home that Christmas after you left, I hadn't paid much attention to you when Linus adopted you, but he invited me over for Christmas, and I saw the most beautiful boy I'd ever seen. You were laughing at something Pride had done. I'd never seen such joy before. I felt like a bastard, but every time you came home, I made an excuse to get a peek at you. The day you graduated, you looked so proud of your accomplishment, and I was proud of you. That night I went back to my hotel and looked in the mirror, fuck, I looked old and—"

"I didn't care about your age, but I wanted to be a grownup when I came back. I needed you to see me as a man."

"I did long before you moved home. So, can we try this again, as equals? Two men who like each other."

"I more than like you, Daddy."

"Ah, there's my bratty boy I adore."

He started to back up, giving Gage a small smile. "You want to come in and have ice cream with me?"

Gage stalked him just like the night in the hotel after their date. "If I come in I don't want ice cream."

"What does Daddy want then?" he asked as he backed through his open front door.

He waited for Gage to speak, but an almost frightening need filled Gage's eyes, and the door slammed. He barely had time to catch his breath as Gage was in front of him, his shirt ripped over his head, and he was in his Daddy's strong arms. It was a frenzy of Gage's boots being kicked off, clothes removed until they were both naked. Their labored breathing filling his ears as his heart seemed to want to pound out of his chest.

When his back touched his mattress, he was shocked. He was lost in kisses and gruff whispers, his cock ached, and Gage wasn't in any hurry to touch him apparently. He pouted, and his Daddy chuckled.

"We'll get there, boy, patience, it won't be long...I've missed you. Supplies?"

"Shit, I don't have...all I have is lube." He didn't bring anyone home, once he returned to Powers it was going to be Gage or no one else at least until his broken heart mended or if it ever had.

"I'm negative, and it's been years."

"Same."

"You ready for me?"

"Yes, Daddy." He'd wondered if he'd like to bottom, but since Gage had fucked him, his toys were a daily thing.

Gage's deep rumble was the sexiest thing he'd ever heard, and he only released Gage long enough for the man to grab the lube from the nightstand. Gage moved to a kneeling position between his thighs and two slicked fingers easily thrust inside.

"Have you been playing with yourself without my permission, boy?"

"Yes, Daddy." The last word broke off on a moan as a third pushed in beside the two. He squeaked as cold lube trickled down his crease.

"Pull your knees to your chest, boy, and keep breathing, nice and even."

The pressure increased to almost pain, and his hole was on fire. He closed his eyes and whimpered when the pressure increased with a fourth finger and then he screamed as Gage swallowed his entire length. He grunted and awkwardly tried to ride Gage's fingers when he felt Gage's thumb massage his rim. Gage tortured his hole and gland until sweat dampened his hair and it stuck to his face.

There was a bite of pain and words fell from his lips, they had no sense nor rhythm as agony and pleasure were swirling together. He kept his legs to his chest but reached down to tug his cheeks farther apart.

Gage swallowed around the head of his cock, and he had no control, he was at the mercy of the man who owned him. Then his system went into shock as it all ceased. His eyes flew open, and he parted his lips to beg, but all that came out was a grunt as Gage took him with one powerful and brutal thrust that pushed him up the bed. He could no longer breathe or think because everything came down to his Daddy savagely fucking his ass.

Gage's body came down on his, and then teeth nipped at his

throat right before his Daddy's big hand wrapped around the front of his throat. Pleasure became an overwhelming mix of panic and pain. He held his cheeks wider, and his fingertips brushed his Daddy's cock with every thrust.

He was owned and used, loved and tortured until reality was an abstract concept. Nothing existed beyond that moment. Gage's fingers squeezed tighter until his breaths were ragged, but he could still breathe. He trusted his Daddy with his life. Gage pounded his gland without mercy until his felt his sac drawing up tight and every muscle in his body tightened, and he opened his mouth to scream, but nothing came out as cum spurted between their bellies.

"Fuck, boy, you were hungry for Daddy's cock." Gage grunted then sunk his teeth into his bottom lip as long strokes became shorter.

He felt the pulsing of Gage's cock against his fingers as the man came sealing their bodies together. It was an odd and powerful sensation as he felt Gage filling him. He dropped his legs to the side, exhausted and sore, but happier than he'd ever been. Gage lay heavy atop him, and he stroked the man's back, felt the powerful muscles shifting beneath his hands.

"I'm going to make you addicted to me, boy."

"Daddy, I already am."

GAGE FORGOT HE HAD A FAMILY

*A*s always, the Trenton Crew loudly yelled around the living room. To make his boy happy he'd finally agreed to come back into the Trenton circle. The last time he'd attended a dinner was nearly a year before, and he was feeling out of place. He'd fought his demons for so many years the fact he was pulling away didn't become clear until it was already too late. Derrick was talking with Pride in a corner and Pride had a mature expression on his face that didn't fit his pre-teen years.

Derrick had shared with him that Pride had a crush and was a little insecure about that. This life was far removed from the one he'd had growing up. Gender identity and sexuality were embraced, he felt like he'd taken his chosen family for granted.

"Still hiding?" Hunter asked from his right.

He turned his head to look at the man and took in the slight wrinkles beside the man's eyes. Time passed too quickly, and he realized he hadn't noticed.

"Not really, just…thinking."

"Would you like to share?"

"Do you have an issue with me dating your son?" he asked.

"Is that what you really want to know?"

Hunter wore his usual smile, and he remembered when Hunter had started freelancing at Trenton Security. Unable to work on the books due to it being a parole violation. Over the years, Hunter had come into his own, no more awkwardness or clumsiness. Hunter had found himself and his home with Linus and Wren. The love between the triad bright enough for all to see.

"Yes." He brought his attention back to the room. "I never felt a part of the team, and it was never more painfully obvious as everyone started falling in love. I wanted what y'all had and felt so inadequate."

"My son is happy and healthy, and while I have my reservations because I know y'all too well, he's a grown man. If you ever hurt him, I will kill you or have my husband do it."

He chuckled because he knew which husband would take him out and he didn't doubt Linus would make him suffer first.

"Do these have something to do with you fighting your feelings for Derrick?"

He didn't even flinch when Hunter ran slightly calloused fingertips over the exposed scars on his right forearm. Since he'd claimed Derrick as his, he only concealed his forearms when he'd added to the already countless scars. He'd carried them too long as his secret shame—a weakness—he couldn't share. Accepting himself was a slow battle but became easier the more time he spent with Derrick and spoke with Kieran. His doctor helped him process it all and realize where his need to harm stemmed from—a lot more complicated than he'd anticipated.

"More the reason behind them kept me from being happy. When I hired on with Trenton, it was a paycheck, a life as far removed from my old one as I could get. It was fine for a while, and then I realized I wanted to belong, but it was already too late. When I saw Poe react to seeing Little in the facility and it was fucking crazy, you could feel the love and pain. That's when I started pulling away."

"It wasn't like we didn't notice. You rarely attended Crew parties or went on runs with us, but each month you pulled back even more. I can see the love you have for Derrick. It's as clear as when Linus and Wren look at me or each other. You deserve happiness, Gage, we all do. Yes, we all have our secrets, some darker than others but none of them make us unworthy of finding love."

As he listened to Hunter speak, he studied the occupants of the room closer. Liv was seated in a big chair with Fielding on his lap. The big, scarred man had prepared to die at any moment with not an ounce of regret. That was until a beautiful blond had given him something to live for and changed everything about Liv. Well, the man was still a huge bastard, but that was just Liv's personality.

Little was chasing his little bow tie wearing cutie around the house while Poe fumed about something. The more pissed off Poe became, the bigger Little smiled. When the big man cupped the smaller man's belly and nuzzled his throat, Poe couldn't remain mad. It proved there was someone for everyone.

Raul was in a corner sipping at a beer as he watched Pure like a hawk. Pure hadn't been the same since the operation ended. The man was losing himself in thought, and he hoped Pure would come to him if he ever needed to talk. He feared Pure's demons were maybe darker than all of theirs combined. His gut told him Pure wanted Raul, but some hidden fear kept him from voicing that.

"Alex was the only friend I ever had, and when I came here, I didn't understand what family was. Peaches and Lily, they were always so adamant to bring us all together. I'm getting there, but it's going to take time."

"And we won't force it but being with Derrick makes you family. Don't fucking think you're getting out of it. I'm not losing my son because you're anti-social."

"Yes, sir," he said as he noticed Linus motioning him toward the back door. Linus along with the rest of the Crew were headed in the same direction as the Crew partners made themselves comfortable on the couch and the floor in front of it. Derrick smiled at him before he went back to cuddling and talking with Pride.

He strode to the kitchen just in time to catch Little disappearing out the back door. His nose wrinkled at the scent of weed as Little and Linus passed a blunt back and forth. Even Livingston added himself to the rotation. He waved it off as it was handed to him. All that shit did was make him tired and hungry, and he had to make sure his boy got home safely.

"How's Cameron and Kray?" Pure asked as he flopped onto an Adirondack chair where Raul took the seat beside him.

They all sat down to face the firepit that Linus lit earlier in the night. He'd forgotten the last time they all sat around after an operation just to reflect, have a few drinks or a smoke or two.

"As well as can be expected. Kray is having a harder time adjusting to freedom. He spends days in his room, and the nightmares wake everyone up in the house with his screams. Cameron is the only one who can calm him down. Alex and Margo set them up with the best therapist. It's going to be a slow process, but to be honest, they'll never be the same, especially Kray."

"Maybe a change of scenery would do them good. Alex is definitely handy to have around." Linus exhaled slightly coughing as he restarted the three-person rotation.

"Actually, he's thinking about it. A slower pace and he can work from anywhere. Margo suggested him and Cameron spend time together. He was away for a lot of her life."

"Make sure you let him know whatever they need just tell us. He's a part of the family now."

He shook his head at Liv's laidback statement. Sometimes the changes in his friends shocked him. Maybe that was more of his issue than anything. Everyone around him grew and moved forward while he was still trapped in his past. He couldn't deny he felt lighter and less tortured by his demons, and he loved the newness of his life.

"How's pet parenthood going for you, Liv?" Little asked with a snort.

"That fucking cat hates me. Who the fuck wants a hairless, blind demon cat? I swear that fucker knows when I pass by and bites me for no fucking reason."

He couldn't help joining in on the laughter. Fielding had wanted a puppy until the boy had spotted the cat alone in a cage. The sweetness of Liv's boy was strange compared to Liv's natural grumpiness.

"Animals can sense evil," Little replied.

"Fuck you."

He relaxed and listened to the conversations going on around him. The squeak of the screen door drew his attention and found the rest of the Trenton Crew filing outside. He studied each one as they made their way across the lawn to take their seats on the arms of the chairs—Hunter and Wren on either side of Linus. The unrestrained affections of kisses and hugs still made him uncomfortable on occasion only for the fact that he was taught that affection was a sign of weakness. Even as he didn't feel that way any longer, he knew he still had things to resolve.

"May I?" Derrick motioned to his lap.

He didn't hesitate to pat his thigh, and everything in him went calm at the weight of his boy. The kiss his boy gave him was sweet and filled with the love he knew his boy felt. He raised his left hand to cup his boy's cheek, deepening the kiss slightly before pulling back. Derrick's parents so close made him cautious about giving his boy the kiss he wanted. He softly nipped at Derrick's mouth before relaxing with his boy's back to his chest.

These nights weren't foreign to him. He'd experienced it hundreds of times since he'd hired on. But unlike the times before, his friends—no, family—were happy with their partners. His boy was on his lap, and he was free to touch and love on Derrick as he saw fit. Part of his brain tried to urge him to be prudent and not to let his guard down too much.

He despised that he rethought his every action, but again, he had more to take care of with Kieran. The cutting wasn't a daily ritual as before. The compulsion was still there and probably always would be in some ways. He couldn't force himself to be something he wasn't, and all he could hope was that his boy would still be there in the not so pretty times.

"Love you," Derrick whispered in his ear as if it were a secret between the two of them.

"Love you too, boy."

He was ashamed he'd forgotten the family that he'd acquired and taken for granted. No longer though, he'd hold onto Derrick and their family. He was more than what Major had made him. More than the scars on his body. And he wouldn't forget that. He'd hold on tight to the bright spots in his life and try to move past the demons and darkness. After almost fifty years of killing himself by pieces, he deserved happiness, and he was going to work his ass off to make sure Derrick didn't regret a moment of their lives together.

EPILOGUE

DADDY KNOWS BEST

"*B*oy, what have I told you about your clothes on the floor," Gage bellowed from downstairs.

Derrick bit his lip to conceal his laughter and his hiding spot. Gage was a grumpy man, he already knew it, but he was a loving yet tyrannical Daddy. They'd been dating or whatever for four months, and they hadn't had any mishaps since the two-week disappearing act. They talked every night about their days, but also what was going on in their heads. He knew some days Gage was crankier than usual and he didn't miss the bloody gauze in the trash, but they were getting fewer and farther between since he started seeing Kieran Dahl weekly.

Gage had shit to work through, and as much as he wanted to help, professional help was best. He'd been a little jealous when he'd met the psychiatrist. Beautiful with long silvery blond hair and ice blue eyes, the man didn't even look real. Tall and super lean, the man would give anyone a complex. He'd heard rumors that the man was making quite a few men and women jealous. The guy seemed super sweet and quiet, but also confident in his job. Kieran couldn't help his alien genetics.

He shifted in bed as he waited for Gage to find him. He'd left a trail of clothes so it shouldn't be long, but if he knew Gage, the man was picking them up as he went. His Daddy was a slight control freak, and his house was uber neat. They hadn't moved in together yet, and everyone was starting to ask when. Most of the Crew members had moved their people in within weeks of dating, but some had known each other for years before getting together. So the living together was understandable when someone pretty much knew everything about the other person.

"I should have known," Gage grumped.

He couldn't help barking out a loud, ugly laugh as he saw his clothes neatly folded in Gage's arms. Gage glared at him, and he rolled his lips between his teeth to muffle the nasally snorting that his laughter became. As soon as he regained control, he moved to his hands and knees, crawling to the end of the bed. "Why do you put up with me?"

"Because even as bratty as you are, I still adore you."

"Aren't I the lucky one?"

"Brat," Gage said as he walked beside the bed.

He yelled as Gage spanked him hard before Gage laid down on the bed.

"Come here, boy, it's time for our talk."

He loved talking especially since he got to cuddle with his man as they did except when he didn't spend the night which it wasn't often that they were apart. He stretched out beside Gage, the man dressed in only sleep pants and he rested his head on Gage's chest. The dark body hair in contrast to the silver and dark gray of his hair. There were a few streaks silver in the mat on his chest, and some sprinkled through the rest of his body hair. He loved how hairy Gage was, and he never hesitated to say so.

"You first," Gage said as the big man stroked his hand over his ass, roughly squeezing his cheek.

"I accepted a job with Linus today."

"Finally, I was waiting for them to replace me in the field, but they weren't hiring anyone."

"Yeah, they waited until Pelter found my replacement. A married man with kids who just moved here. The city wasn't working for him, and as he got older, he wanted a new quieter place so he could spend more time with his family. He hasn't passed the Crew Test yet, but that should be fun."

"Yeah, we're not much on law and order, no matter how many times Pelter has threatened to arrest us."

"You next."

"Move in with me."

He jerked his head up and rolled to his knees to stare at Gage. "Are we ready for that step?"

"You're here anyway most nights, why pay rent at your place?"

He let out a long sigh and batted his lashes. "You are so romantic."

"You're asking for a spanking, and you're still bruised from your paddling two days ago."

He wasn't going to admit he enjoyed the correction way more than he should, but the last one wasn't his favorite. He'd left the house without his vest on, and Gage had found out. He had court on a day he'd asked off, so he was just coming home afterward. Gage was obsessive about his safety. That's why he was surprised when he hadn't fought him joining Trenton Security. But in some ways, he guessed it was different—crew watched crew, and also Linus had strict rules, and Gage would be there to watch him if needed.

"I want to move in but are you ready to have me around all the time? We still spend some nights apart to have space."

"I love you more than I have anyone in my life. I want to wake up to you every morning. Have our talks in bed before we go to sleep. A wise man once told me, *You gave him a symbol of promise. A physical vow of your care and affection, isn't it cruel to make him wear your ownership and not claim the right to it?*"

"He does sound very wise. Pure right?"

"He is the sanest one of us, and that's not saying a lot."

"I love you too, and I'd be honored to move in. I won't even make a mess on purpose to get spanked."

He chuckled as he was pulled onto Gage to straddle his thighs. "But I want you here more than anything even if you can't pick up after yourself. Tell Daddy you'll move in."

"Yes, Daddy, I'll move in."

He was flipped onto his back, and Gage's firm lips came down on his. He moaned as strong hands circled his wrists and pinned them above his head.

"I promise, I'll never hurt you."

"I never doubted that. You're not him."

Those were the last words they spoke as Gage drove him insane and as Gage slowly pushed into him, the man whispered his love, and it was everything he'd ever dreamed of. All Gage asked was he love him and trust him to understand Daddy knows best.

THE END

ABOUT THE AUTHOR

J.M. Dabney is a multi-genre author who writes mainly LGBT romance and fiction. They live with a constant diverse cast of characters in their head. No matter their size, shape, race, etc. J.M. lives for one purpose alone, and that's to make sure they do them justice and give them the happily ever after they deserve. J.M. is dysfunction at its finest and they makes sure their characters are a beautiful kaleidoscope of crazy. There is nothing more they want from telling their stories than to show that no matter the package the characters come in or the damage their pasts have done, that love is love. That normal is never normal and sometimes the so-called broken can still be amazing.

Trenton Security

Livingston

Little

Gage

Pure (Coming Spring 2019)

Masiello Brothers

The Taming of Violet

His Everything

3 Moments Trilogy

A Matter of Time

Killing Him Softly

The Men of Canter Handyman

Black Leather & Knuckle Tattoos

Chance at the Impossible

Not For the Likes of Him

Bloody Knuckles Bar & Grill

Clipping the Gargoyle's Wings

Cold Beer & Afternoon Naps

New West City Universe

Co-written with Davidson King

The Hunt